B. D. Pedersen

My Name

Is

WICKED

Edited by

June Pedersen

ISBN-13: 978-0692262191

ISBN-10: 0692262199

Prologue

All my life I have been a hard worker and achiever. When I entered this career choice, I took my chosen professional personality and applied it as it should be applied with complete dedication and commitment. Over the years I have managed to survive, becoming one of the best contractors and most feared contractor working the world's industries.

To be a contractor one must be diligent and dedicated to his duties. It's your reputation at stake and nothing can be permitted to damage it. You make your reputation by the results you show when carrying out a contract. If you survived the competition then you could demand higher payoffs and benefits. I had achieved that level. None were above me in both reputation and results, but many have tried and many more will.

In actuality it's an animal type of industry. You receive a contract and you take whatever action it directs and you complete it in the proper time span and then move on. You learn to keep your feelings separated from the job. Emotions do nothing but get you killed.

If others died during the implementation of the contract, that was business. That's not your problem, it's theirs. No one is going to intercede for you. You're on your own. The fact is most contracts required just that kind of action, someone has to die.

The best part of this job is it's all legal. If you were a contractor working a bonafide contract, then the laws did not apply to you while you were carrying out your contract. That's the way it had to be and the way industry wanted it to be. After all, they were the ones who hired the contractors and they had specific targets they needed to be dealt with. Any interference from the law was not acceptable. If there was collateral damage, then there was nothing that could be done.

Collateral damage does happen and the system and process take it into account. Competition between sides can result in the, innocents getting hurt and some dying.

That would prove to be the payoff for what was about to happen. I was to be drawn into a contractual situation that would cost me dearly, if not my life. It was a setup, and I was setup as the prime target in this game of cat and mouse. However, there would be a lot of collateral damage on the way. I don't know if it was planned this way. All I knew a lot of people were going to die. The fact was a lot of people had already died.

They made one fatal mistake, they tried to place me in the role of the mouse and it would be their downfall. They tried to put me into a maze and let me run around until I ran into death. You don't do something to Wicked. It's a form of suicide, know what I mean.

I was a loyal contractor, but when my contract placed me on the receiving end and was in fact a trap, then all bets were off. I didn't know who the hell did this to me but I was going to find out. Then I was going to show them what being a mouse was really like. I can be and am a wicked man. I do things to people, no one can understand why or what my reasoning is.

I would spend time determining how I would take someone on and then the means by which I would dispatch them. Did I enjoy it? Not really. I enjoyed a successful completion of a contract and it was all that was important. But how I killed was almost as important because it left a message. A message if Wicked was after you, you were dead and your death would be most wicked.

Yeah, this time someone had over stepped. Someone had pushed the line and they were going to pay for it. I was walking waist deep in bodies of both my friends and others, but that was not going to stop me. I would find out who it was and in time I would have them.

But who, who the hell was behind this crazy thing going on in the Detroit region? Who the hell was making the power plays that were responsible for the death of all those business executives? Who was bringing in the cream of contractors to try and stop me or take me out? If they were playing war games, they were sure as hell making it real and permanent.

No this was special; this was something that took all the rational of this crazy world we are living in and turned it all around. This was so crazy it could easily kill the world and all it has accomplished over these many thousands of years, and I was sitting right smack-dab in the middle of it. My life was on the line and I either solved the puzzle or tomorrow would never get here.

I have dodged a lot of bullets over my years as a contractor, but this is something entirely different. It seemed at every corner I turned there was a round coming at me and behind those rounds were the men and women I had worked with over the years. When it comes to relationships, they take the back seat to money, and there is a lot of money on the line right now.

My name is Denton Wicked. That's right, you heard me. Wicked, that's my last name. I have been a contractor for many years and I have not gotten this far in this violent career path without learning something, that being, when working a contract, you had to be ruthless and wicked as hell. Anything goes and nothing is taken for granted.

It would take everything I've learned, found out, developed and stole to achieve a favorable ending to this current contract. A whole new realm of reality was about to come into my life and I either adjusted or I died. If nothing else, it makes for a good story.

Chapter One

Meet Wicked

Pain can be a real puzzle when one is trying to discern just how badly they are hurt. For me pain was something I was able to cope with. I mean I had to have some real serious pain before it made an impact on me. I guess what I'm trying to say is I have a high tolerance level for pain.

Pain is an odd assortment of feelings that reach throughout your body telling you just where something is wrong or going wrong. But, it's not the only application of pain. No, it's even more rewarding when pain is directed toward someone else.

For me pain comes in a series of events, a process where something happens and the resulting pain tells the story good or bad. In this case it was the round from one of my opponents that first hit me. It is part of the job and one learned to expect and accept it. You can feel the round coming in by the amount of wave concussion it created at the leading edge of the round.

Yes, the round is moving at several hundred feet a second, but you're attuned to the feeling of rounds coming in on you and moving by you. Then there is the initial impact of the round as it hits flesh, your flesh that is. In my case it was a heavy blow, something like someone hitting me with their fist right on the outside of your thigh.

There is no sense of ripping or tearing into the flesh, it's the sudden impact of the round as it hits. It tends to deaden the area of entry for a fraction of a second. In this case the round passed right on through which is not always the case. Whether it passes through or not depends on the shape of the round.

A round from a hand gun usually has a round or concave nose which causes the round to start to break up or mushroom. When the break up happens, it must pass through the material of your clothing before hitting the skin and then tears its way through the body.

12

This will almost always result in the round stopping somewhere inside the body. It does not have enough inertia to drive itself and any material it may have gathered on through the body. That becomes a major issue for the wounded.

On the other hand, a round from an assault rifle is shaped much differently. They are usually metal jacketed and pointed so when they hit, they drive through the material with less tendency to accumulate fibers from the material. They also carry more than enough inertia to pass on through the body or leg in my case.

That initial hit has little pain. For me the pain comes after the numbing of the initial hit, that's when my tolerance for pain is to my advantage. In other words, I can function with minimum interference from the impact of the round. Believe me when I tell you after being hit a number of times you grow accustomed to taking another round and your tolerance builds.

The average man would be withering off in some corner by now, but I'm more than able to continue on. Besides, if I gave up now, I would pay the ultimate price for my weakness. No, I would put up with the pain and continue fighting as long as I could. Someone had to pay and I was determined to see it wasn't me. Unless a round hit me heart center or between the eyes there was going to be hell to be paid by someone and in short order.

It had been a foolish move on my part that put me in this predicament in the first place. All the years of training and witnessing the same foolish moves by others, and still I fell for it. I guess it could have been worse, he only hit me with one shot and he fired three times. All right I screwed up but that's not the end of it. I still was in fighting shape and it meant I was still dangerous as hell. Yeah, in short order he was going to find out.

Damn, I had called this confrontation myself and expected to be on top of everything taking place. Now I was on the defense and I hate that. I prefer to be the attacker for the simple reason I feel it gives me control over the situation and conditions I am working in. With him now holding the offense I feel more like the prey and not one who holds his own destiny in his hands. Yeah, I made a simple mistake and walked right into a round.

No, that's not acceptable to me. So, I'll have to do something about it. His next move will be the determining factor in this game. If he does it the way I think he will, I'll have the offense back on my side in just seconds and he will be the one at deaths door. Think. I had to keep thinking no matter what the hell is going on. Calm down and slow time down and make each rational decision as the situation demands. Work him, he's yours.

My wound is bleeding a lot, but it's not a fatal wound. It's more a hindrance than anything else. I need to get the bleeding stopped and then get back to business. The one good thing was it was a thigh wound and it went through and through, lots of blood but no serious damage. Right now, I needed to slow down and calm myself and let time ease me into the next move. He's worried and still does not know where I'm at and for that reason I had him.

I managed to get the hole plugged and then a bandage wrapped around it. That stopped the bleeding for the most part and I felt I was in good enough condition to take this fight to the finish. This one I wanted badly; he was about to pay dearly for going to the gun. All I needed was one bad move on his part, and if I'm right he thinks I'm in a worse way than I am, and he'll get careless in his desire to finish me off.

Yeah, there he is. I can feel him coming. His lust to kill me is driving him and he's not thinking. He has me and it's just a simple case of finishing the game. Yeah, he's coming and the game is about to end. That is his mistake, he's thinking about the game being over.

He's looking ahead at what he will be doing once he's done with me. Such a simple process, move in and locate and then plant a round into the back of his head. Damn, I can feel him thinking, and he's plain crazy, crazy as hell.

I can feel him breathing and moving slowly step by step. His guns at the ready and he's tensed up looking for me. He knew where I was twenty seconds ago, but now he's not sure. I couldn't have moved too far wounded, so he must be right on top of me, just on the other side of this crate.

I rolled over on my side with my back flat up against the crate to make my profile as small as I could. I centered my gun at the edge of the crate nearest my head and held my breath. I had one chance and one chance only.

When he moved around the end of the crate, I had to hit him and hit him hard with everything I had.

My adrenaline level was off the charts, and my pain level was zero. Everything was centered on the corner of the crate and I knew he was right there just on the other side of and around the corner. I could see the air movement from his breath as he approached the corner. I could feel him tensing up as he prepared to move around the corner and take me out. He was right there and ready.

I knew once he was in place and ready, he would move out from behind the crate and center in on me. I needed to have him sighted and the hammer dropping before he could pull off his first shot. It's all timing, every bit of it. The only guess work was when he started his move, and I was good at guessing. Yeah, there he is and he's started his move, all or nothing.

I started to pull off my first round just as he started around the corner of the crate. As the hammer fell, he moved directly into the path of the bullet and it hit him just above the groin area and below the bellybutton. Damn that had to hurt like hell and he showed it. A flash of fear shot across his face followed by an expression of amazement knowing he had screwed up.

I adjusted my sight and pulled off two more rounds hit him dead center and down he went. Poor bastard didn't have a chance. He figured I was helpless with the first round, and made the mistake of thinking I was the average Joe and I would not be able to function once hit.

He was wrong, dead wrong. He was looking at the payoff and what he could do with the money once this job was over. He lost his concentration and for that he paid the ultimate price, screw him anyway.

The past three months had been hell for me and everyone else associated with me. I had a contract to determine what had happened to a man, employed by those who had hired me, to find him. It was a no-big-deal issue.

The worst thing that could have been involved was a little industrial spying, and it is exactly what it was, except it was not little and it was not a no-big-deal issue, it was as big as any one thing could ever be, and I was dead center in the middle of it. In fact, I was the sacrificial lamb in the overall plan they had set in motion.

My name is Denton Wicked. Yes, you heard right, my last name is Wicked so don't make a big deal about it. The only thing I will caution you about my name is I can be wicked, as wicked as they come. In my business there is no room for anything more acceptable than the basic fundamental mindset it's the other guy who dies and I don't care how. I don't give a damn how I do it. All I know is I will be the one walking away.

I'm a trouble shooter and I mean that by every conceivable meaning of the term. I investigate, determine the cause, find the one responsible, and then settle the issue permanently. My employer, a large business interest, whose name is unimportant at this time, contracted with me to protect its interests in this particular issue. Needless to say, there were millions if not billions on the line and in those situations, no one plays good guy. The most brutal will be the one to win and that is why my name causes even the bravest to have second thoughts.

It's not my place to determine which side is right or wrong. I am a hired mercenary or hired gun, if you prefer. The side who gets to me first with the most is the one I will accept as a client. In this case I was approached by one client and the offer made was acceptable to me and the contract was set.

Mind you, I am expensive, but I guarantee my work, to finish it no matter what. If I'm on my last leg, I will finish it, trust me on that. When I have a contract and I come at you I don't stop, I don't compromise, I don't care what you are or who you are the contract will be completed.

There is only one exception to any contract I agree to. I am the sole judge as to who is right or who is wrong. If the side I contract with is found to be lying to me or using me as a screen to cover their action, then the contract is off. Damn I hate that kind of a situation in a contract.

It doesn't end there though. At that moment, when and if I discover their transgression, they will pay and not in a monetary sense. They will pay for putting me at unnecessary risk, for lying to me in the first place, and for determining I was a sucker for their action. No, they will pay and it will be hard line and wicked as hell.

As a contractor I stand outside the normal social order. I am of a world outside in which all others live. I am judge and jury and my decisions are final even unto death. You step on me and I'll tear your leg off and then while you lay there bleeding, I'll deliver the rest of my message right between your eyes. Get me!

I stood there looking down at my opposition noting he was a rather young man. He was good, but not quite good enough. The other thing was I didn't know this one. I knew every mercenary out there, but this was a new one. It could have been his first job or else he was a sacrifice, a means of drawing me out and setting me up.

That cold, you're in for it now, feeling shot through my body as I dropped spun and dove for my refuge behind the crate that had saved my life. The first two rounds hit on both side of me as I hit the floor and continued rolling across the opening between the rows of crates and the wall they were stacked against.

They had sent a hit squad after me and I now knew I had it all figured out. I knew right then and there wicked was the game, and the means by which they would pay was going to be nothing any of them had seen before. But first I had to deal with this squad and that would be my pleasure.

Yesterday I had received word the primary contractor for the opposition was planning an assassination move on me. With me, I never ran from something like this but take it head on. That is the only way to address something as deadly as this, go right at them and kill anyone and everyone involved.

The word was I was being followed and I would be led into the storage facility down by one of the long-abandoned loading docks by the river. I had to admire the way they were trying to set me up. Everything had fit perfect with what I had been doing the past three months. Yeah, they were filling in the blank spaces for me and what would come out would be the biggest industrial war yet.

That's when I called my opposition and told him I would meet him in the warehouse down by the river, the old one south of town. Why let them think they had this thing planned, no they needed to know I had them figured.

It's the details. That was the means of surviving in this business. Know the details about everything you are going to do and be involved in, the details of this warehouse were no different than the details of your adversary and those who hired them. I doubted seriously those in the hit squad knew anything about this place. All they knew was, I was there and they had me.

What they didn't know was this old warehouse had a history. A history that was in my favor and in turn gave me the edge. This warehouse had been built in the early 1920's and had been a storage facility for the bootleggers of that time.

Bootleggers, that was a nice name for the mob, gangsters who built this place and used it for their movement of the liquors they were smuggling and selling. They were in to making money, a lot of money and thanks to the prohibition laws of the time they were making more money than they knew what to do with.

That resulted in the building of this warehouse by one of the biggest gangsters in the whole of the United States. It was a time when corporate America was struggling. These individuals recognized a market and took advantage of the demand for alcohol of any kind.

What no one knew or had forgotten was those people knew how to build in ways and means of getting out the building in the event the government showed up to raid the place, you know escape routes. The place was honey combed with escape hatches and tunnels. A lot of them had fallen into disrepair and had collapsed over time, but a few, the more dependable ones were still there and still usable.

Now just how the hell did I know that? Again, it's all in the planning, the knowing what is ahead of you and how it fits into your plans. I have not survived all these years through pure dumb luck. No, one learns to weigh the odds and if possible, weigh those odds in one's favor. Come on start thinking. Yeah, I knew this place, hell I have used it for years and it has served me well.

I had spent time learning the history of this place and then made a few clandestine trips here to find and check out the passage-ways that had been left behind.

It was a place with planning behind it and good planning at that. For me it was the perfect place, as long as I survived the initial contact, they had me set up for. I have to admit the hit squad did catch me off guard. I had planned on the meeting to be just a one on one and not a sacrifice.

That's why you plan, why you have alternatives to fall back on. That's how you survive in this business. Now it was my turn. Now the beginning of the payback begins. And it won't stop until a good portion of the industrial might of this region is laid waste.

But first things first, I had this group to deal with and deal with I would. I knew there were two others out there and they were on opposite sides of the general warehouse area. I also know most hit squads were made up of five people, usually a leader and then his doers. I needed to find the leader, he would be the first to find his way out of here and back to hell.

The leader, where would he be right now, right here in this place? I thought back to my initial encounter with the first trigger man. He came at me from the front of the warehouse and to my right. That meant he had moved down the right-side alleyway between the stacks of crates. I was relatively sure he did not know back against the walls there was room for a person to move between the wall and crates. The original designers of this place had put a walkway in that area which would give anyone moving through the walkway cover from the crates.

So, the first trigger man came at me by the right, my right side, alley way. There was also a left side alleyway, my left side as well which left three lines of crate storage about thirty to forty feet wide running the length of the building.

At the front end, facing the street were two large entry doors big enough for the movement of large freight crates by even larger fork lifts. At the river end were two identical doors used to transfer the crates to the dock for loading onto ships.

Back when it was built it was used in that way but more as a cover for the actual business that went on here. Now it was clearly just a storage warehouse and the back dock doors were no longer used.

So, there we were in a face off inside this huge ugly old warehouse. It was dark outside so the inside of the building was spooky as well. What lighting it did have was grossly lacking. Enough though so we could target one another and see where we were going and what the others were doing.

I knew there were at least four others out there and I had two located within an area of the building in elevated positions affording them good fields of fire. The other two were still not located and identified. I felt fairly comfortable the leader was still at the main entrance to the building. That left the fourth shooter's location unknown.

I felt relatively sure the fourth shooter was a rover and he was the one who was actually trying to track me down. He was just like the one I had just dispatched. Only he was working the left side. I made a quick check around me to see if I was leaving any trail he could follow. No, I was doing well, the bleeding was not a problem and I was leaving floor marks to the minimum.

I moved back toward the front of the warehouse and settled in to wait for the rover to come to me. That way I could watch for the leader as well and get an idea as to where the other two static shooters were located. It wasn't long before I could smell him and then hear him. The guy was scared to death. He knew he had to find me and he knew who I was and what my reputation was, that's where the scare came in.

Ten minutes passed and there he was not more than an arm's length away from me. He needed to take two or three more steps and then I could reduce their numbers by one. He did it. He took the two steps I needed, something I would have never done because it moved him toward me and the stack of crates I was using for my cover. I let him slide just past me and then reached out and slit his throat and then drove the knife into the back of his head just where the spinal column meets the skull. There the blade smoothly slips up and into the brain. He died quietly and quickly.

Now I wanted the leader and I moved ahead toward the front of the warehouse. I had him spotted before I got to the front of the building. He was just inside the door standing in the shadows with his gun at the ready and watching for any movement. I saw him reach up and press his throat mic and then stand there. I was sure he was trying to call the man I had just finished off.

I could tell he was not happy and he was getting more and more nervous with each passing second. I stood there and settled in to wait for the team to come together again. He now knew he had lost two of his people and he wanted the others to regroup and then take me on as a single combined team. It would never get that far.

I heard them before I saw them, both coming, one in each alleyway as they approached the front of the building. The leader brought them to him and the three of them stood there talking the situation over. They were nervous as hell with their heads turning and looking every direction possible to try to ensure they were not taken by surprise.

Too late, I was there just marking my time when I would do the whole bunch in, but right now I wanted them to suffer. I wanted them to know they were in a losing situation and there was nothing they could do to change the inevitable.

Evidently, they felt they were in a safe location because they started to relax. When the hell will these people learn there is never a moment when one can relax? Hell, I had them but I was not relaxed. I still had that feeling there may be another, one who was not with them but was there for the same reason. One who was waiting for me to make my move and then he would make his.

Yeah, that was it, a sixth one was in the building. One who was not known to this team, but was there as a backup, as an extra measure to ensure they got me. Yeah, he was here and I could now feel him. That small essence of his presence was all around me. I needed to deal with him first and then these pigeons would follow him to hell.

He was close by, just as I was to the three waiting to die. This one was just as close to me. I reached out searching for the tell tail marker that would identify him and locate him. There he was just feet from my position and he had not spotted me yet. Wicked little man, you're going to die now and so will the others.

I planned each shot taking into consideration each of the characters I was dealing with. The lone and extra shooter had to come first. He was the most intelligent one of them all, and would surely react more quickly and in all probability, his reactions would be right on the spot.

Next would come the two snipers, their reactions would be faster and more direct than the leader, but not as on target as the first one would be. Last would be the leader. He's a leader but that does not mean he was a good fighter. In all probability he was not that good a fighter and he would freeze.

I gave myself ten more seconds to zero in on the shooter and then braced myself and went for it. I fired the first round and started to set up on the other two. The first round hit its mark and took the shooter down. It was a perfect shot and one I knew would pay off the biggest. The next two went in quick order leaving the leader standing there with his hands in the air looking around for my location.

I stood there watching him and letting him stew in his own brew. "Hey man, it's nothing personal. Let's let it end right here right now. You go your way and I'll go mine and I'll guarantee we will never meet again, all right?"

I couldn't help smiling at the proposal he was making. Hell, yes it was only business and I still had some business to carry out. I let him stand there looking around knowing full well it would come any second. "Come on man, it's all over. You took everyone down and doing the same thing to me will gain you nothing. Just let me walk and I'll tell my boss we got you. It cost me my entire team, but we got you."

I had to agree with the guy and he was doing one heck of a job trying to sell me on his option. The only problem was I had only one option and that meant he would not be walking out of this place any time soon, no it would be never.

I slowly raised my gun and targeted him and then calmly pulled the shot off. He dropped like a brick. I left my position and cautiously approached the shooter and confirmed the kill. I then moved to the front entrance and checked the two snipers. Next was the leader and he was a confirmed kill as well.

I then moved over by the pedestrian door and opened the panel next to it and set the system. I immediately moved back and to the east side of the building and found the trap door, opened it and dropped through. I followed the tunnel out from under the building and out beyond the road running in front of the warehouse. The tunnel tied into a storm culvert and I exited the culvert a block from the front of the warehouse.

I moved across the field and up onto a dike area and then moved back to a position across from the warehouse and settled in to watch. I was maybe a hundred yards away.

It was twenty minutes later when the first car pulled up in front of the building. Three men got out and walked to the open door of the warehouse and looked in. Obviously, they had seen the bodies lying there and one returned to the car and made a call. I knew they were not police and also knew they were from my contractor, well my x-contractor.

By now the head of the company was being informed of the situation. They still had a problem and it was a big problem. One thing these people don't like is failure, especially when failure jeopardizes them.

More cars pulled up and more people were milling around out front of the warehouse. Finally, the last car arrived and a single man left it and walked over to one group of people. He then walked to the front of the warehouse, looked in and then turned and started shaking his fist at the other. Clearly this guy was pissed off.

I reached over and pulled the tarp off of the control box, opened the lid and reached down and pushed the lone button on its face. The whole of the front end of the warehouse went up in one huge cataclysm. Along with the cars and the people standing outside. I would say that was a fine mode of passing on my declaration of war toward those who had crossed me. In one move I have taken out almost their entire upper level of security.

I'm sure it wasn't good news to the president of the corporation. He had spent a lot of money only to have his entire strike team lost in one huge explosion. Now the fat was really in the fire and he knew he was next. This game had gone on long enough and it was time to finish it.

Chapter Two

Back to the Beginning

In this day and age the world is run by industry. Where governments once stood, industry now runs the show. Slowly but surely over the last one hundred fifty years industry had worked its way into the day-to-day operations of the governmental duties that had been performed by politically based governments for all the history of the world.

People had become fed up with the issues of politics and the power games the politicians were always playing. People were tired of sending representatives to their respective government capitols and only getting lip service and no real representative actions from those they elected. The political parties were in on everything and it was all related to what was best for the party.

There is just so much people will put up with before they finally have had enough. It was the same for industry, the producers of employment across the world. In time the two, the people and industry took up the issue and politically based government came to an end. In some cases, violently and in others they went out with a whimper.

Government succumbed to the never-ending pressure and infiltration of business into their operations and duties to their countries. Industry worked their way into representing the core needs of the people and provided the expected duties of government, eventually replacing the faltering governmental bodies.

That does not mean politics had gone away. No, it was still there in the operations of industry and inter and intra relationships between the many industries who had taken claim of the territories they functioned in. One could not say industry did a better job. They just had the balls and capabilities of displacing governments. When the people were finally fed up with the current state of affairs, it gave industry the ability to make the move to remove government from the scene.

The people as well became more of a working class. No more middle class, just the upper class and the working class. There was not even a poor or down and out class. You either were of the upper industry-based class or you were a worker. Anyone else, within the system, didn't survive. It's not that it was a bad system, it was just the ability to move up, to advance, to become something greater than your parents was no longer there. If you managed to move into the upper industrial class it was by selection and not your skills.

As with any move as huge and involved as this, the people really did not understand or realize just what they were trading off for. Once they saw it, well it was too late. The power mongers who ran industry now had the political system of the world by the throat and the politicians would not survive. No, it was not a communistic form of governing, it was industrial. Everything that took place, which was built, designed, or developed was for industry and its operations, it is a profit-based system.

Yes, they still had the support element, police and fire services who provided services to both the people and those of industry. There were still Doctors, Lawyers, Restaurant Owners, Mechanics, Grocers, Builders, and all the other professions that existed, also known as small business, they were there and functioning as before.

The people lived well because the industrial brokers knew a well fed and pampered work force was easier to control than one, that was dominated. As a result, there was little or no resistance to the takeover by industry. A void had been developed and industry filled it.

In addition, a well fed and cared for working class meant the demands for industries products would continue to be in demand and increase in demand. It was a true supply and demand system and industry had set itself up to run this system.

However, this does not mean there were no other classes, there were a few of us who lived outside the class stratification system. We were the special interest group, those who carried out the special and highly dangerous needs or wants of industry. It was a segment of the population whose primary purpose was to maintain the status quo, to maintain the position of industry in relationship to the people and the relationships between the individual industrial regions.

We were an element of the social structure who carried out the will of the industries we contracted with. It was this class who were the ones above the law, who worked outside the reach of the law. These were the dirty little doers who ensured the position of each industrial giant who contracted with them, the ones who carried on a clandestine war that never ended but ensured the status quo across the whole of the Earth.

We took each contract individually and fulfilled the conditions of those contracts to the letter. One's reputation was built by the skill in which they fulfilled their obligations to their respective industrial contracts.

In carrying out those contracts there were no rules, no obligation to society. As I said before there was no civil or criminal law. We are immune from any legal action against us no matter how much collateral damage is brought upon society. It was an all-out competition between the contractors for one industry as opposed to the contractors for another.

Regions all across the world had developed based on the major industrial activity present in those areas. Detroit was again the auto industry capitol of the world. Every auto manufacturer in the world centered their business there and built their empires there.

Technology, data and information control had focused in on old Japan and all technological industry had centered their business and all other related activity there in Japan and the Far East.

The same was true for all the other industrial processes across the face of the world. Steel, electronics, furniture, weapons and weapons of war, drugs, both illegal and legal, oil, shipping, timber, and the list goes on. Each industry dominated in a specific geological region of the world and this in itself has become a problem.

The whole of the world's national boundaries changed. Recognized nations of fifty years ago were now gone and in their place were the industrial regions that populated the world. These problems often resulted in industrial wars.

The old national boundaries that used to exist were now replaced by industrial boundaries. This resulted in more than one industrial center being located where a nation had once existed. Here on the North American Continent, there were five industrial regions with each region maintaining their own respective border.

It doesn't take long for a young person to figure out they had no future other than what their parents had. It's not that the working class did not have a good life. The fact was they had a great life and could do just about anything they wanted when off the job.

Their salary base was good and that meant they had an ample amount of money to spend for purchasing the necessities of life and the luxuries as well. From a health perspective they had hundred percent health coverage. Industry needed a well-cared for working class and so they saw to it no one lacked in that area.

It reminded one of the old Socialist System, you know cradle to grave coverage or care. The only difference was the Socialist Political Systems used military force to maintain their dominance over the populace. Under this new system the individual did not have to live as a worker and that brought about the third social class of this new system.

The Outlanders were those who did not want to live under the control and guidelines of industry.

The Outlanders were those who scavenged and lived off the throw off or discarded leftover from the worker class. No one was concerned with the Outlanders. They lived as they wanted as long as they didn't violate the laws. If that happened then they were dealt with harshly and without regard for their future, in other words they were executed. They lived and functioned in the shadows of society, and as long as they stayed out of the way and did not make themselves a problem to the system, they were left alone.

But it cost them as well. Being an Outlander meant they had no medical or social assistance at all. They could receive no benefits from the overall social structure. Where they lived was their choice as long as it was out of the way of the overall social system. That's why they were called Outlanders. They lived in the prairie regions or the mountain regions of the world.

So, we had the Industrial Class, the Worker Class, the Contractors and the Outlanders. What a system, but it worked.

I had determined early on I had little choice in my future and had decided I didn't want to be in the Worker Class nor the Outlanders Class. I was locked out of the Industrial Class, so I opted to become a freelancer. A gun for hire, A Contractor and eventually the highest paid and most in demand Contractor on earth.

It had not come easy. Each and every contract had been a trial and test of my resolve to continue on. I learned early on survival depended on one's ability to set their feelings aside and do what was needed to win and to survive. I earned my name recognition and the name Wicked became a hallmark for something that was really wicked. Clearly the odds of me surviving to become one of the top contractors across the world were slim at best.

As a unique class of people in the world, the contractor was the one person who could work for any industry or company willing to pay the price. This meant with in one contract you could be on one side of an issue for a particular industry or company and the next contract you would be on the opposite side you were on in the prior contract. It is a profession based on reputation and trust. If you lack in either you were dead either physically or contractually.

It was almost a self-governing system in that if you became known to be untrustworthy you would not be contracted for jobs by the industrial system. This was a deadly system, if you became branded as untrustworthy or lacking in ethics you might as well be dead, and in a short time you would be anyway. Once seen in that vein the best you could do was to work under a Contractor as a Subcontractor and it was the Subcontractor who was thrown to the dogs when the most hazardous jobs were to be addressed.

Over time I became the one contractor everyone would look for first. There were others who were as good, but none were as dedicated and committed as I was. Once a contract was signed, I would fulfill it or die trying. There were no compromises if you were on the other side from me, you were targeted for death.

Yes, I knew many of the other contractors. As a matter of fact, when not on a contract we would often share an evening or night out with one another. I had several who I considered good friends and they looked at me in the same way, but we also knew we could, at any time, find ourselves on opposite sides of a conflict and when in that position there were no holds barred. We knew and accepted it. It was all business and nothing more. That's why we never ever talked business when together.

Sounds deadly doesn't it, and I can assure you it is. The bottom line was this, we placed our lives on the line and we are paid a substantial fee as a result. If we were successful, we usually lived. If we failed then the odds were good, we would die as well. That was it, a simple black and white issue.

The Industrial Regions didn't care. All they wanted was a successful processing of their contract with you, nothing else. If they lost in their contract bid then your welfare meant nothing, they wouldn't use you again anyway. The turnover rate was considerable to say the least.

It was three months ago when I got the call. It was from one of the founding industries of the industrial system. It was clear from the beginning they had a major issue developing and they were trying to get a jump on the other regions before they ended up being on the receiving end of whatever was cooking.

My initial meeting with the industrial client was through a lower management operative. He laid out the basics of the issues and advised if I decided to accept the project, additional details of the issue would be made available to me at that time. I reinforced my basic rules of contracting and he agreed and took the data to be passed on to their lawyers for further determination.

This process was normal and at this time I saw no issues that would indicate there was something far more involved here than I knew. There is a certain level of trust that develops between you and a prospective customer. I had dealt with this particular customer a number of times in the past and it was always above board and right to the letter of the contract.

Three days later I was again contacted and invited to the corporate office of the company for a final sit down on the contract and awarding of the project. Everything was moving along just as they always had and I felt good about this particular contract. Not only did it look lucrative for me, but it was a project that should only take one or two weeks. The pay for this time period was off the charts. That should have been a sign to me, but I let it pass.

The contract meeting lasted less than two hours and as I left the building, I had in my hands my future financial security for the next twenty years. It was a rather simple contract, but one that was also delicate and full of pitfalls.

It started out as the usual industry to industry spat. Some upstart company had aligned itself with one of my client's biggest challengers. It was going to be my job to contact and convince a company owner he had made a real error in aligning with my client's primary competitor.

Considering the contract, my actions would take two directions. If the target agreed to the issue and changed his position then it would be my job to escort him or them to my clients for the signing of the agreement papers and to provide protection for them in the event their prior and x-partner tried to do any harm to anyone from the target company.

This was a normal contractual process; one I had done time and again. That should have sent up red flags for me, but I felt this was one of those major issues that needed to be addressed fast and the industry did not care what the cost was. Apparently, their future profits were projected to be extensive.

The other option was in the event the target company owner refused my approach; I was to remove him from his position with his company. In other words, he was to be terminated with prejudice.

Now before you jump to a conclusion, this is not the mob as it was known in the years past. That mob had been exterminated years ago. Nor am I a mob hit man. It just so happens this is part of my job, the elimination of people who oppose the goals of the industry I have been hired by. This is a cutthroat business and from time to time it requires drastic and deadly actions be taken.

Yes, it is murder, but again it is not illegal. Remember, the law does not apply to issues of conflict between industries and the contractors they hire to carry out their contractual needs. We and our actions are exempt from the law. It is all part of the industrial competition that exists in this day and age.

What I didn't know was I had been set up and it would take everything I had to determine what was going on with this

48

contract over the next three months. I guess I had better fill you in with a little more detail on this whole thing. Then you will understand why and how I dealt with this mess.

It was November 10, 2273 and I was basically out of work. That did not mean I was in financial straits, it only meant I had not had a contract for some time. Things around the world were rather peaceful at this time. The relationships between the industrial regions were going well and that usually meant people in my line of work were not needed. My needs for living were not a problem and frankly I was enjoying the free time.

There was, and it was normal, the usual bantering between the different industries over regions of control and patent issues. All of those usually meant they would fight it out in the industrial courts and leave the violence outside.

Times of difficulty usually came about because of proposed or actual acquiring of new, and sometimes old, companies coming into a union, combining with or being taken over by one of the larger regional industries. The competition between the controlling industries was heavy and could easily result in open conflict.

On the surface, the CEO of the industrial regions in conflict maintained a working relationship with one another. In all their relationships there was no display of any conflict between them. Basically, it was business as usual with the attitude their representative contractors would work the issue out between them. Within the corporate world they were above those activities and never let them enter into their mutual relationships.

Odd, well from your perspective I would agree. If one were to step back and take a long look at this process you would see the executives of the conflicting industries carrying on a normal relationship, even enjoying a round of golf during the process.

Yet under and behind that façade was the actual battle that was being fought and decided. There was a line we were never to crossed, and that was the direct attack on the industrial leaders themselves. That was off limits. Any deaths would be those of the opposing contractors and no one else. That is where this particular contract was different. It would be this difference that would spell my success or failure and ultimately whether I lived or died.

Overall, the need for a contractor was clearly there and we were the ones who dealt with the violence issues. The benefit to everyone is it avoided open warfare and the fighting was restricted to those professionals in the service of each individual industry. This was the situation I thought I was getting into with this new contract.

At the signing of the contract, I should have realized there was something more to this, but you know how it is. I hadn't had a contract for some time and I was getting a little restless. I like to be working and when I'm just sitting around it's a waste of my valued time.

Anyway, I had the contract and now all I had to do was find my target and then make a move on him and present my client's offer. So, I started my research on the targeted company. The name of the company was Saturn Futures. What the hell kind of name was that anyway?

It was a fairly good-sized company and that in itself was interesting in that it was only five years old. The owner and president of their board was one Bradley R. Worthington, who had founded the company. He held the largest stock holding for the company. He had a board of eight individuals, all members of the company. There was no one on the board from outside the company. In fact, after further research, I determined there was no public stock offers on the company it was an in-house holding company.

That gave me a feeling there was something much more involved in this. I set that aside and concentrated on locating and setting up a meeting with Mr. Worthington. This would prove to be a project all in itself. He was one hell of a person to make contact with.

You would think it was simply a matter of making a call. After all, the Saturn Futures building was right next door to Detroit Industries, the company I held the contract with. Hell, they could have done this themselves and save them one hell of a lot of money, another flag I let slide by.

It took me a week to finally come up with a phone number that would take me to his corporate office, so I made the call. It was the normal receptionist answering the call and when I requested to be connected to Mr.

Worthington, she obliged by passing me on to his executive secretary.

I had been this route before. It would go one of two or three ways. I would get an automatic answering system that would give me a number of options which I would select from and then be put on hold to wait. The other method would be a live person whose sole job is to irritate the hell out of me. Just then I got number one. "Welcome to Saturn Futures, Mr. Worthington's Office may I help you?"

That was nice. She had a pleasant voice and one I had heard before, many times. Yeah, it was an automated answering system. I sat there waiting for the message as to which button to push to get whatever individual or location I was looking for, but it never came. I then asked. "Is this Mr. Worthington's Office?"

"Why yes sir, it is."

This was different, I would swear I had tied into an automatic answering system, but she responded to me. "Would it be possible for me to speak to Mr. Worthington?"

"May I ask the nature of your request?"

That was reasonable. "I am inquiring about the services of Saturn Futures and so far, I have not been able to find out if your company can provide me with the services I need. I have been referred to Mr. Worthington for that reason."

"Yes sir, may I have your name please?"

All right, now were moving. "My name is Denton Ashley."

"Thank you, Mr. Ashley, please hold for a minute."

That was it and she left the line. I sat there waiting for her to come back and after ten minutes I had a strong feeling I was not going to hear from her again. I decided to hang in there. With a man as busy as this Worthington, it may be difficult to run him down so I gave her the reasonable doubt and waited.

All things come to those who are patient and after fifteen minutes the secretary came back on the line. This time she was cold as an ice cube. "Mr. Worthington will not be able to speak to you at this time. If you have any questions, he asked that you present it to him in the form of a letter. Thank you and have a good day."

That was it. She hung up and I had just wasted twenty minutes of my time. I guess the phone system or process wasn't going to work, I was going to have to make a one on one with this guy. That would mean I had a lot of research to do on Mr. Worthington and the levels of security he had working around him.

One does not simply walk in on the head of a company and start a conversation. These people are hard as hell to get a one on one with and when you do it usually means you had to work the system in order to gain the privilege.

Security for the head of a company, no matter what its size, was vital here in this time. Anyone foolish enough to try and operate a business and think they didn't need security was not long for this world. No, he would have security and it would be heavy, that I was sure of.

I would spend the next week doing my research on Mr. Worthington. I had no doubt in my mind what I was about to enter into was going to be hazardous and above all, most difficult. There was something nagging me, trying to tell me this was not just a simple contact and convince type of job. No there was much more involved here and I was sure I was the target and not Mr. Worthington.

It then entered my mind, if this Mr. Worthington was so difficult to contact and my preliminary investigations found little information on him, was there actually a Mr. Worthington? That shed a whole new light on the situation. I was starting to see red flags all over the place. What I didn't see was the fact the flags were pointed at me, not at Mr. Worthington.

So, what, it made no difference what kind of threat was coming at me. I would move ahead and take on whatever stood in my way. I had been this way before and I knew what I would have to do. If they thought for a second a brush off was going to take care of me, they were about to learn a whole new lesson in life and its greatest challenges.

First of all, I needed to know what Saturn Futures really was all about. My preliminary investigations shed little light on this company. So, I found it necessary to start over and to carry out an in-depth investigation of Saturn Futures. This was not moving along right. I was beginning to feel I had not been informed on a number of issues that were just now becoming evident to me.

So far there had been enough strange and odd issues popping up I knew I had better pay attention and be ready for just about anything. I had not ventured out for any formal one on one contact yet, but it was coming and I had better be expecting the worst and not let my guard down. What had started out as a simple one- or two-week project has now become a situation totally steeped in a fog and lack of information.

It took me another week to gather all the information I could find through public access on Saturn Futures. As it turns out this was not a financial institution but was a developmental company that was putting together a system and means of approaching the planet Saturn and settling colonies on its satellites.

That changed everything I now was looking at something involving the highest levels of industrial development and research, the value of which was worth more lives than one can imagine. This was huge and my contractual pay off would take far more than I had anticipated. The levels of concern were now moving up the chart and I knew my new contract was far beyond what had been related to me.

This company was in the process of designing hardware that would be used to develop ships to make the journey to Saturn and to make landings on specific satellites for the purpose of setting up colonies. The second thing I discovered was the equipment would be produced to achieve this goal could also be used in military applications here on earth.

Now things are starting to get touchy. There was far more to this than I was led to believe and I was starting to believe just maybe I was going to find myself in the middle of something I didn't want to be in. I needed to locate and meet with this Mr. Worthington.

Something was wrong here and I had better go on alert and start paying attention to what's going on around me. Survival always depends on one's ability to watch for and spot trouble before it reaches you. I had it figured out, but not to the degree I should have.

Three days later I was sitting at my favorite bar. I was frustrated and frankly a little down. In my research to learn about and find Mr. Worthington I had so far come up blank. That is not normal for me. I was missing something but it was still eluding me. I was still somewhat puzzled by what had happened so far and I was sure there was a whole lot more under the surface than I had been led to believe.

Damn, I was beginning to feel frustration and if I didn't come up with some answers, or at the least, some leads to those answers soon I was going to have to get down and dirty. That I didn't want because it meant I would be escalating this issue and this usually resulted in a counter move by my target.

This particular bar was considered a safe zone for contractors here in the Detroit region. You could find just about anyone you wanted to find in this place and there was no threat of a confrontation. How the place had become a safe zone I don't remember, it had been one before I came into the practice. It was a self-governing place. By that I mean, if you carried out business here everyone in the place would turn on you and you would be retired permanently.

I had just finished my second drink and ordered the third one up when someone sat down beside me. I glanced over at him and there sat Chad. Chaderton Wheelright a fellow contractor and one I had worked with a number of times in the past. I wouldn't say we were the best of friends, but if one can have friends in this business then Chad was one of mine.

I turned back to the bar as my drink was being set in front of me. "Chad, what's up?" I was looking at him through the mirror on the back side of the bar.

By this time the bartender had moved over to him and he ordered. "I'll have the same as my friend here." He was also looking at me through the same mirror.

He turned to me. "Denton I was just out running around and saw you here and thought I'd stop by and see how things were going."

He was trying to be nonchalant and relaxed but was doing one hell of a poor job of it.

Damn, he was never good at lying about anything, I could see through him so easy it bothered me every time he did it. I turned to him. "Chad, that's a bunch of bull and you know it. Now what are you here for?"

These people don't just show up and I knew I had screwed up coming to this bar after starting a contract.

It's not that I feared any kind of an event here. Chad wouldn't dare carry out any action here, it would end his career. No, I was sure things were just what they appeared to be, a casual meeting and nothing more.

His drink arrived and he picked it up, took a drink and then turned back to me. "Denton, you're right this is business. I'm here as your friend to give you a message. The word is you've got a contract out of Detroit. Well, I'm here to tell you to drop it and pull out. It'll be the only warning you're going to get, understand?"

As I turned to him, he set his drink down on the bar and turned facing me head on. "Chad how do you know I've got a contract, let alone out of Detroit?"

His eyes were focused on mine and he was serious as hell. "Look Denton I have my ways and you know that. The issue here is you're working a contract that's not acceptable to my client and you are being asked to pull out."

I have known this man for a long time and I knew him to be a tough contractor. I also know him to be honorable and he would never violate a contract he had taken. No, this situation had gotten really bad and I needed to pay close attention. "Chad, if what you say is true and I had a contract, any contract, you know I can't do that, drop out of it. Hell, if you were in my shoes you would say the same thing, so what the hell are you doing here?"

I could see the frustration slip across his face as he tried to keep the issue quiet and between the two of us. "Denton, listen to me. You have been pulled into something you don't want to be in. I wouldn't be here if it weren't for your best interests, I'm taking one hell of a risk being here."

He was right, this was a visit by one professional to another to try and stop a bad thing from getting any worse. I knew right then and there; Chad was on the other side. If I stayed the course, we would be facing off somewhere down the road. What the hell should I say to him anyway? Damn, this was not getting any better.

We both sat there looking at the mirror behind the bar and watching the people moving around behind us. I knew Chad never worked alone like I did. He had backup and they were somewhere in that crowd of people behind us. The question was, were they ready to take action against me here and now? Damn, he wouldn't do that, this was a safe zone and any contractor who violated any zone would place himself in a far more serious situation than just one of opposing contracts.

Chad must have seen my eye movement as I scanned the people behind me. "Denton, I'm alone. I didn't bring anyone with me. I'm here because I care about you and I wanted to give you an upfront before thing got out of hand. You have to pull out. You're in a bad situation and it's going to be worse day by day."

Hell, I appreciated what he was doing and saying but he knew I couldn't do that. He was actually here for himself, for his own conscience. All right, I can understand that and I think he was being sincere, but it changes nothing. I had a contract and I would live or die by it.

I still wanted to know how he knew my contract was with Detroit. "Chad, how do you know about Detroit? That is upper-level security and the only way you could get it is if you were tied to Detroit yourself. Are you playing both sides Chad?"

He waved me off and finished his drink, slipped off the stool and then turned back to me. "Denton, I just know, and this is the only warning you're going to get. Back off, if you don't then you are going to pay the ultimate price, understand?"

That laid it out all right and I understood completely. I nodded my head. "All right Chad you've delivered the message. Thanks for the heads up and I hope to hell we don't see one another anytime soon. If we do Chad, I'll defend myself, got me?"

He stood there looking at me and nodded his head then turned and walked away. The line had been drawn and we were on opposite sides of a most difficult situation and I still did not know all that was going on. It was time I found out.

If you're confused by now, let me tell you so am I. First of all, no contractor ever comes to another and warns them to pull out of a signed and enforced contract. Second, no contractor has or knows the contractual condition of another contractor. That is, they may know a contract was being worked, but they did not know who it was from. That is something not given out by anyone.

Now when the action starts it's obvious both sides know who is working for whom. But until then the only ones who know who is working for whom are those who have the particular contract with a particular company.

Somehow, he knew and that was not right, not in the least bit.

My years of experience are now telling me this whole thing is far more complex and involved than I had thought. Now I was starting to feel like I had been suckered and that is one feeling I hate and will not tolerate. If it proves to be true, then more than just a little hell is going to cut loose around here.

My next issue was getting out of this place in one piece. The bar itself was a safe zone but outside that door it was not. There was a good chance Chad and his team would be waiting outside the door for me to leave the bar and then it was no holds barred.

There was always the back door but I knew any contactor worth his salt would have that door covered as well. Damn I should have left with him and then I would have had cover and could have defended myself. I needed a group of people and started to watch the crowd.

The battle lines had been drawn and at least I now knew there were some lines, and who was standing on which side. I knew the moment I stepped through that door, and onto the sidewalk outside, I would be in enemy territory. I also knew there would be at least one other contractor out there and possibly more.

Ten minutes later a group of eight to ten people started to head for the door and I left my seat and moved in with them. We moved out of the bar and around the corner and into the parking lot. Fortune was with me; they were parked near my car. I had made it to the car and now needed to clear the lot. I let two of the cars run interference for me as we hit the street.

I was right, there were two cars waiting down the street for me. As I passed by them, I saw one of the occupants of the first car point at my car and say something to the person next to him. By this time, I had checked the entire street out for traffic and other players in this game. Traffic was moderate and I saw no other cars that could be involved.

I did not see Chad in either of the two cars. They were subs and that meant they were probably newbies or contractors with little experience, which would be in my favor.

As soon as I passed the first car I swung into the inside lane and punched it. I knew I needed at least ten to fifteen car lengths head start on them if I was going to be able to get out of this mess. Chad had set me up just fine. I had to give him credit for having the balls to come into the bar and sit down with me. I should have known he was setting things up, but I guess the booze had slowed me down.

I saw both cars pull out from the curb and accelerate while trying to get through the other traffic and into the same lane I was in. They had to force the issue and that caused the other drivers to break and slow their move on me that much more.

I hit the first intersection and took a right across the outside lane just missing the car beside me and slipping ahead of the car behind that one. That left my pursuers with another traffic snarl to work through and it gave me time to get to the next turn. I made a left and then took another right. I kept the left and right turn pattern going for the next six blocks and cleared the area successfully.

At first, I thought I had made it but then one of the cars came around the last corner behind me. The lucky part was it was only one car. I had lost the second one. Now I needed to end this thing as soon as possible and turned into the first shopping mall I came to.

As late as it was, the mall lot was empty. I made a U-turn and brought my car to a stop. The following car came onto the lot about ten seconds after I got stopped and they came right at me. It was going to be a drive by and they were going to hit me with everything they had. All I had at the time was my .40 and I was going to have to make that work.

I set myself up so I could swing my car to the right just before they got to me and set myself up for a clean field of fire on the front driver's seat. Timing, that was going to be the key to this one, I had to move at the right time so they could not take evasive action against me and it still give me time to target on the driver.

I took a deep breath and slipped forward and to the right and then dropped my arm on the window ledge and targeted in on the driver and opened up. I hit him with everything I had and as fast as I could pull the trigger. My rounds tore into the front window and side window next to the driver with several rounds hitting him before he could respond.

I let the car move by me and kept firing and raking the side of the car as it came by. They never got a shot off. I hit the gas and pulled away and turned around, dropping my spent clip and loading the next one up. I came in on the back of the car and moved right coming alongside the passenger's side and opened up on them again this time raking the passenger side of the car. The best I could tell there had been two people in the car and I nailed them both.

I swung around again and came up to the car on the passenger's side back of the rear door. I sat there watching for any movement. After a few seconds I left my car and approached the other and found both men inside dead. I needed to get the hell out of there and went back to my car and headed out of town, taking every turn that came up to ensure no one was following.

Chad had warned me and set me up at the same time. I knew now I was in a total war and whoever was financing this thing was going to hit me with everything they had.

Well, that's the way this business is. You can depend on anyone who talks to you like Chad did were actually against me. I had a feeling it was just getting started. If Chad was involved then there were others. Now I was figuring this mess out and I didn't like it. This was going to be the toughest contract I had ever had. If I survive it, a lot of people will die in the process.

That's the contractor business. You never know what a case is going to turn out to be, but in this case, I was the prime target. It was all set up to take me out and end my career.

Chapter Three

Total War

Here I was, I had already been working this new contract for three weeks and all hell was busting loose. I couldn't find this Worthington dude and now I had been warned to pullout or die. That was emphasized with an attack as soon as I left the bar. You don't have to tell me twice, once would have been just fine. Damn I hate it when I'm in the dark like this. Well, that was going to change and change now.

Information is worth more than gold or diamonds, it's worth everything you value and right now I needed information and was willing to sell my soul to get it. That was well and good but on the other side people spent untold amounts of money keeping others from finding or discovering their information.

Once I had been visited by Chad, I knew I was way outside the information channels in this thing. It was obvious he knew a hell of a lot more than I did and that put me at the worst disadvantage. When I made the contract, I thought I had been briefed in full concerning the job to be done and any issues that may be involved. It now appeared I got nothing near what I needed and I had better correct that as soon as possible.

It was now Monday afternoon and I was sitting outside the Detroit Industries building watching the personnel moving in and out of the building. I was watching for the right one to show his face. When he did, I was going to introduce myself and we were going to spend some private time together. It would either be easy or hard and that would be up to my guest. With me it made no difference at all. I was going to get what I wanted and whether it was the hard way or easy way made little difference.

I was watching for one individual I had seen when I was at the Detroit Industries building signing the contract. He had been outside the office where the signing had taken place and my contact had gone out to talk to him while I read over the contract. I noted this person was looking right at me and pointing at my contact while talking to him. That was the person I wanted. He was behind the scene and he probably had a lot of the information I felt I needed.

It was just five minutes after five when he showed. I knew I had the right guy as soon as he cleared the door. The way he opened it and let others pass through ahead of him. The way he walked and carried himself he was the perfect target for me. Yeah, this was the right guy all right. All I needed to do now was to contact him. Well not really, I was going to kidnap him.

I watched as he walked across the street and started down the sidewalk next to the park. I drove around the block and came up on him from the front. There was no one else in the area and I pulled over. "Hey mister, could you help me?"

He looked over at me then looked around and pointed at himself and then bent down to get a better view of me. "Oh Mr. Wicked, what can I do for you?"

I pointed down the street. "Is the main office at Detroit closed already I think I left something in that office when I was there. At least I think I did. I had it with me when I came but I can't find it now.

He started walking toward me looking off in the direction I had pointed and then moved over by my car and placed his arm on the door. He leaned down and looked at me starting to say something when his nose met my .40 caliber barrel square on. He froze. "Now open the door slowly and get in. Don't yell, don't try to run, and don't try to take my .40 caliber from me."

He nodded and opened the door and got in and sat there looking at the open end of the barrel. He was trying to say something but nothing was coming. "Shut up and sit back. Get the seat belt on and sit quietly. I'm not going to hurt you, but we are going to talk. Understand?"

Poor damn guy, he had no idea what was going on, but in short order he would. All he was to me as a source of information I needed and needed now. He would give me everything he knew. He may not know how this was going to turn out, but he would, I can assure you he would.

He was nodding his head as I spoke and then was able to get a choked response out. "Ye Yes sir, I, I understand."

Perfect, I had my source and now I needed to get back to my office. Well not a real office, a place. You know a place where I can work and not worry about being interrupted.

Heart to heart talks, are not always the best way to go, but with this one I felt this was the way to take. I spent a lot of time finding the right person for our talk and now I needed to take the next step. Just the ride alone would do more to loosen up his mouth than all the devices in the world.

It took us twenty minutes to get to the old house and into the garage. As the door closed behind us, I advised the man to relax and not to try to be a hero. I was a contractor and he knew what that meant. He again nodded his head as I got out of the car. On my directions he did the same.

We got into the house and I invited him to sit down at the kitchen table and I went to the refrigerator and got a couple of beers. I placed one in front of him and then sat down across the table from him and opened my beer.

This particular house was a throw away house, you know, one or two uses and then you burn it. That leaves little or nothing for other contractors to home in on. In effect it leaves a dead end sitting there in front of them.

The kitchen was not unlike most. It was old with a single light hanging from the center of the ceiling. The shade for it had been discarded years ago and all that was there was the one lone light bulb.

The table sat directly below the light giving anyone sitting at the table a clear and well-lit view of everyone else at the table. My guest was about to learn it was also a great location for a face-to-face talk, whether he wanted to talk or not.

I motioned with my beer for him to take his and drink. He at first hesitated and then picked the beer up, opened it and took a long drink. As he set the beer down, he looked back at me. "What's your name?"

"John, John Stanford."

"Well John I'm sorry for the way I picked you up but it was for a good reason and in the near future the fact I forced you to come with me to this place will ultimately save your life."

He was nodding his head and then took another drink from his beer. "John, I need some information and I think you're just the guy who can give it to me. What do you do at Detroit Industries?"

"Please mister I can't say, I can't tell you that."

"Sure, you can John, just open your mouth and start talking, that's all it takes. On the other hand, if you don't then I'll be forced to make you open your mouth and start talking, do you understand?"

This time when he picked his beer up his hands were shaking so bad, he had to use both hands just to get the bottle to his mouth. "Yes, sir I understand, but I took an oath."

Great I picked an honest man. Damn the luck anyway. "John, you're making things really hard on me. I can see you're a good and honest man and that means I will have to extract the information I want and it is going to be hard on you and just as hard on me. But I'll have to do it."

He set his beer down and I could see the resolve building in him. "No sir I cannot tell you anything."

I shrugged my shoulder and got up and went over by the stove, opened a cupboard and pulled out a hammer, a pair of pliers, a screw driver, a wire cutter, two sixteen penny nails and a box of stick matches. As I set them on the table his eyes grew bigger and bigger.

He was starting to stammer as I sat down and started to rearrange the tools. "Now wait a minute here. You're not serious about using those on me, are you?"

"John, I need this information and I'm going to have to get it out of you anyway I possibly can, know what I mean?" I was now holding both the sixteen penny nails in my hand looking them over.

His eyes were riveted on those nails when. "Look, I don't even know your name?"

His voice had a quiver to it and I knew I needed to be a little more relaxed and not as aggressive with this one. He was also a liar. He had used my name when I first contact him.

"It's Den."

He cleared his throat. "All right Den I have a wife and kids and I need to get home to tonight."

That caused me to smile, hell it was just another day at the office for him. "You have a good family John?"

"Yeah, I do and this will kill them if you harm me."

"Gees I'm sorry John, but if you're not going to cooperate with me, then I'm forced to take other actions. Look John relax, this is just information I need, that's all. It's just business and not personal. I need it and you have it so if you're not going to give it to me then I'm forced to take it from you. Get me?"

I felt sorry for the poor bastard. Here he was heading for home and along comes this idiot and the next thing he knows he's kidnapped and up to his ears in trouble.

"Now John let's get this over with so you can return home to your family and I can be on my way. Now tell me, what is Saturn Futures all about?"

He finally picked his beer up and took a deep breath. "All right I'll try and answer your questions, but you're putting me in a bad way you know." He took another drink and then started. "Saturn Futures is a company that has invented and built a new power plant for interplanetary travel."

I sat there looking at him and thinking, a new power plant for interplanetary travel, that's good. "All right John and what is so big about it anyway?"

"Sir you don't understand. This new power plant is capable of huge power generating capabilities. If used here on earth to drive fighter planes or ships or land tanks, nothing could match them."

He paused a moment. "If the power plant were placed in a cargo ship it could cross the Pacific in less than two days and the size of the plant would be about the size of a V-16 gas engine."

That caught me halfway into a drink of beer. I coughed my beer out sending a wash over him and then stood up and ran to the sink. I stopped and turned. "The size of a V-16, you're full of shit."

"Yeah, I'm telling you this unit is so powerful a small unit the size of a two-cylinder motor could operate a house's electrical power needs for a year on one tank of fuel."

Oh boy, now it was starting to make sense. No wonder Detroit Industries was interested in this company. If they controlled it, they controlled the world. Nothing but nothing operates without some driving power and if Detroit Industries owned that level of power production, they could name their own future.

Crap, Saturn Futures was the Holy Grail and more than one industry would go to war to own and control it. Detroit Industries was trying to get a jump on everyone else and they were using me as the side show, a diversion so to speak and the game was just getting started.

Chad was right and now I knew who he was working for. It was the same bunch I was working for, only I was being hung out to die.

I sat there looking this John in the face and trying to determine what my next move should be. Was I going to send him on his way to his family? Was I going to eliminate him and leave his body some place never to be found? Or should I just lock him up for a while until I have this whole mess worked out?

One thing I was sure of, I was mad as hell and getting madder every second. They had set me up as a diversion and when that didn't pay off, they were now going to eliminate me. I could see it coming a mile away. On top of that they had hired one of my best friends to do the job on me. Damn this thing was nuts, crazy.

I turned to John. "What is your position at Detroit Industries?"

"I work in Engineering. I'm a junior project manager sir."

"All right I'm going to give you my phone and I want you to call your wife and tell her you have been tied up for a few hours and you'll be home soon. Now John, hear me carefully if I find you have been lying to me, I will hunt you down and kill you right on the spot wherever I find you. Got that?"

He gulped hard. "Yes, sir I do."

"All right now, call your wife and let her know you've been delayed and you'll be home shortly."

He took the phone and made the call and advised his wife just as I had directed him.

"Now John, I'm going to take you back to your neighborhood and let you out. You need to know ten minutes after we leave this house it will go up in flames and there will be nothing left of it. If you notify anyone you were kidnapped, I'll know about it and you know what will follow. Got that?"

"Yes sir."

"All right let's go."

I drove John back into town and dropped him off on a street corner and then drove away. My next stop was my primary safe house. I needed time to figure this thing out and prepare for the coming action and there was going to be some coming action.

For the next week I continued my research on both the Detroit Industry and the Saturn Futures company. So far everyone has been able to keep this thing under wraps, and the longer they were successful in doing that the more time I was going to have to set this thing up. I knew this much, I had to make things so hot any further consideration about taking me out would be so far down the list it would become a non-happening.

If I was able to do that then I would be relatively free to hunt down those who had set me up and deal with them. As a contractor I cannot afford to be treated in this way and let it ride. Any future contracts would never happen if I let that happen. No for my own reputation and future I had to deal with this. What I didn't know was when I did it could be the catalyst for a worldwide industrial war.

What a system, what a useless damn system this whole thing was. If anything, right came of this it would be the death of this system. I could only hope, but the odds of that happening were nil, this I was sure of.

It was the first week of month two when I noted the car behind me. I knew immediately I was in trouble when it came up on me. They were not being discrete in any way. They had a purpose and it was me and I'm sure I knew what they were planning.

I played it cool for the next block so I could get some idea as to how many I would be dealing with, it was three. A driver and two-gun men, all right, so now I had to figure how I was going to handle this. A street fight was not in my favor. No, I had to take them somewhere so I could deal with them permanently.

At the next intersection I took a left turn and headed out of the heart of the city and into the suburbs. If I could get them to move on through this area and out into the country, I had a chance. I knew where I wanted to go and what I wanted to do. All they had to do was stay with me.

Now I knew the company had brought in more than just Chad. These were newbies and they were raw as hell. All I needed was to get them to the place I wanted and then I would be teaching them a few lessons on what being a contractor was all about.

I could tell they were getting impatient as I approached my selected destination. I chose an old drive inn theater I knew of. It was in a fairly isolated area and any gun play would be muted by the high fence around the theater.

As we came to the main drive to the front gate, I hit the gas and made the turn. They jumped on me just as I expected them to. I drove through the gate and headed for the concession stand in the middle of the theater. I needed to get their driver in a driver-to-driver position with me and so as I approached the concession stand, I headed left and just as I hoped he headed right to try and cut me off from the rear gate.

As I came around the stand, he came up on my driver side and I had the driver right where I wanted him. As he came by, I concentrated on the drivers head and opened up with my .40. It was perfect and the car veered off past me bouncing over the car mounds and heading for the main screen. Someone managed to get control of the car and open the door and dump the driver out and then start after me.

I had moved back behind the concession stand and was waiting for them.

No matter which side they came on I had a plan and this time it was for the replacement driver. If I could take him out it was a one on one and I knew I had the last man as well. Wicked little boys, they thought they could take Wicked out and now they were learning a lesson of a life time, a short life time at that.

As they made their second pass, I was able to bring the shooter into my sights and opened up on him. I missed, but a round found the driver and that ended his new career as a driver. The car slammed into the side of the concession stand and I pulled up right behind it. The shooter, who was now alone, was out cold in the back seat. I opened the back door and drug him out and to my car. I tied him up and put him in the trunk of my car and left the area by the back gate.

My destination was an old warehouse down on the waterfront about half an hour away. I pulled into the warehouse, which was still being used as long-term storage and drove to the back. Did I mention I owned the warehouse? I had owned it for about fifteen years now. I kept the ownership under a false corporation with no ties to me.

I hit the remote and as I entered the warehouse I drove to the back of the building, hit the remote again and parked the car behind some crates, got out and opened the trunk. The shooter was awake now and his eyes told me everything.

I pulled him from the trunk and drug him over to the door and then down under the warehouse. I had found a small room down there years ago and it came in handy for this kind of activity. I tied him in a chair and took a seat on the other side of the table from him.

We sat there looking at one another. "You work for Chad?"

He remained silent.

"Do you work for Chad?"

Still, he said nothing.

Finally, I leaned forward. "Let me tell you something about me. I've been in this business for many years. I know just about every contractor out there and I know their moves and preferences. You're not the first I've met this way and you're not going to be the last.

"Just two weeks ago I had a talk with Chad and I know he is contracted out and I know it is a contract opposed to me. So, when you and your boys came after me, I was sure you were from Chad. So, you're not really letting anything out of the bag, just confirming what I already know. Now, are you from Chad?"

Finally, he started to nod his head. "Yeah, we were to take you out this afternoon before 5 o'clock."

"What does 5 o'clock have to do with this anyway?"

He sat there looking at me. "I don't know. All I know is he wanted you dead before 5 o'clock."

I was trying to tie that time in with my research but it just wasn't working in. "What will happen if you fail to do that?"

"He told us not to come back."

Wow, Chad was playing hardball and these guys were being sent to the slaughter house. "Did Chad say anything that sounded nuts or crazy to you?"

That was a strange question and he looked at me like he didn't understand. Then it hit him. "Yeah, he did. He said something about having your ass out of this before the first of the month. And that 5 o'clock would tell them he had achieved his goal."

I stood up and paced back and forth in front of him about five times and then moved around behind him and pulled the .40 and put around into the base of his skull. I then drug him out on the pier and dumped him in the river.

I returned to my car and headed back downtown. Something was about to happen on the first of next month and I only had two days to figure it out. I was sure I was no longer under contract with Detroit Industries, so I could do as I wanted, and I wanted to find out what was going on and get in some payback.

Right now, I had confirmation Chad was after me. That meant he would be using a hit team if this latest attempt failed. I couldn't control that, but I could control the location of the hit or action. It had been years since I had taken out a hit team, but I felt I could do it this time as well. I knew Chad and I knew how he worked. He seldom used highly experienced people in these teams. They cost him too much. No, he would bring a team of newbies to the party.

Still, I didn't like the idea of being targeted by a hit team. That meant the word was out to other contractors as well and it may not be something I really want to be involved in, not at this time anyway.

No, the gloves just came off and it was Chad or I and I had a strong feeling it would also include one or two other high-level contractors. There was something extremely heavy involved here and that meant money and power. Detroit had hired me for a job that was of no importance to them. They already controlled Saturn Futures so why the hell did they need me.

The obvious answer was they needed a scapegoat. Someone they could hang out in front of all the other industries and feed them a line as to the dastardly thing I had done to the head of Saturn Futures. Yeah, that was it. They had done the Saturn Futures Chairman of the Board in and needed someone to blame.

A sacrificial lamb, that's all they needed me for. Those no-good SOB's and for that they would pay and pay dearly. This was now a whole new game and I was not going to stop until I had my blood and they had nothing. These people seem to forget contractors have no allegiances. Everything is business and as the business goes so goes the actions of the contractor.

As far as I was concerned our contract had ended and now, I was going to give them a graphic example of what happens when you enter into a false contract and sell the involved contractor down the river. They want blood and its blood I'll give them.

I guess the thing that was bothering me the most was they had planned this all along and I had been specifically selected to be dumped into this position. That was not going to happen. If there is one thing a contractor, especially this contractor, holds on to is their reputation, and mine was spotless. I have never neglected or violated a contract in my life and no one and I mean no one is going to violate one on me.

I cannot impress on you just how determined I have now become concerning this whole situation. There was something deep and ugly going on here and it was a lot more than just me and some violated contract. No, I was the diversion and the real show was scheduled someplace else and without my input or involvement.

Now I needed to know the full story, everything that is sitting behind the scenes. These people were into something deep and they were going to use me as their cover. When they go this far and take the top contractor to use as the stooge, then it was time to tear a new hole in the good old normal operations of this system.

One thing I would let them know as I put each of them away was, they started this thing and I was going to take it all the way to the end. It was time to teach the industrial giants who the top dog contractor really was. In the process, there would be a bunch or new industrial heads moving up to fill the vacancies I'm going to leave behind.

Chapter Four

The Game Gets Dirty

It's one thing to work on a contract basis for these industrial regions, but it's all together something else when they, the industrial region, set you up in order to achieve some targeted need of their own. That's when things get out of control and that's when things need to be corrected.

First things first, and that is Saturn Futures. I need to get into the place and determine what the hell it really is and why Detroit Industries would carry out such an unbelievable action as they appeared to have done.

There was something strange and dangerous happening here and if I planned on surviving the next few weeks, I had better find out what it is.

I knew this much; Saturn Futures had developed a new power plant of some kind that could result in huge advancements in travel and power generation. If that were true then whoever held control over Saturn Futures had the rest of the world in their grip.

A device like this, as in the past, can change the balance of power and growth across the whole of the world. If it does fall into the hands of one company, then that one company could rule the better part of the world in short order. This whole situation had now become a balance of power game and when something like this happens the body count goes up and no one is safe.

I was fairly sure the other industrial regions around the world would never stand for it and the resulting industrial war would quickly expand into a world war. This was clearly and quickly moving out of control.

Second, I had been tagged as a subterfuge, a false target as a means of pulling everyone's attention away from Saturn Futures and concentrating on me. If I could run fast enough and long enough, then it would give Detroit Industries the time it needed to take Saturn Futures over. In a way that was a great strategic move on the part of Detroit Industries. They knew full well I would be nearly impossible to corner and take down. If it happened, and it won't, it would take weeks and not days, ample time for them to move.

Third, one of my contractor friends had been offered and given a contract on me. That action in itself pissed me off, the fact was one of my so-called friends had accepted the contract. Yeah, it's only business, but you would think there would be some level of loyalty there. When I think about it, he did come to me and he did warn me. It still didn't feel good.

Now I needed a plan. I started to go back over everything that had taken place these past few weeks. I had been contacted by Detroit Industries and offered a contract which I accepted. It had been a normal negotiations process but it only took about two hours to complete.

As I think about it, they were not their normal penny-pinching selves in the negotiations. They agreed to everything I wanted. I should have seen the signs, they were flashing bright red.

I walked out of those negotiations with the most lucrative contract I or anyone had ever seen. Of course, I did, they never planned on paying off. Damn their hides anyway. For that alone I was going to make them pay.

So why me, they could just as well hire some nondescript newbie and send him into the battle. No, they wanted this thing to be high profile and having half a dozen hit teams chasing me all over the countryside would draw a lot of attention away from Detroit Industries and give them time to make their move.

What the hell anyway. I would be running all over the countryside with these other contractors after me? Crap that was stupid. They had to know I would figure this thing out and then I would come after them. I would end up targeting Detroit Industries and that would draw attention right back to them.

No, that didn't fit. There was something else here I was missing. Yes, any action involving me would draw a lot of attention, but not that much. Industries spend millions tracking the activities of each other and a localized battle between me and some hit teams would in no way impact the normal tracking operations of the industries. There was something else and I was missing it and missing it big time.

I need to stand back and take a look at the big picture. First of all, Detroit is a huge area with no less than twenty auto and other transportation industries located in the region. When you consider the geographical size of this region, you're looking at an area equivalent to the old states of Michigan, Wisconsin, Illinois, Indiana, Ohio and the Providence of Ontario from before the industrial regions came into effect.

In time every highway, railroad, airline traffic route started and ended here in the Detroit Region. They had direct ties to the Oil region and major construction regions throughout the country and world. This was one hell of a big place and behind it stood fully twenty-five percent of the gross financial holdings of the world.

Then you toss in the Saturn Futures and it doesn't make sense. In comparison Saturn Futures is nothing compared to Detroit Industries. They could swallow Saturn Futures up in seconds and no one would be any the wiser. Overnight the entirety of the Saturn Futures organization could be exterminated and replaced with a regional puppet.

It then came to me, I had to get into Saturn Futures and I needed to do it as soon as possible. I shifted everything I had to concentrate on Saturn Futures and gain entry into that facility. I started an in-depth study of the company. I needed everything I could find on it and then some.

Next, I needed to case their building and determine their level of access security and any areas of weakness that may exist. One thing I knew above all else, nothing but nothing can be made impregnable. There is always a weakness and that was my target.

Getting into a place is one thing, but that is not the only means of gathering information. Being able to access their onsite data or computer operations is the other means of gaining the information one wants. That was one area I excelled in and so I set up to begin an electronic break-in as soon as possible.

All right I had three targets to work on. The first one was the overall company information resources and that target I started after right then and there. I began with a general internet search on the name Saturn

Futures. That alone brought up some interesting issues.

Almost immediately I learned the name Saturn Futures was not their original name. Its original name was PowerHouse Industries. All right, so what does that tell me? Right now, nothing, almost every company out there has changed its name from time to time, some more than once. That brings up the next question, what's in a name?

I decided to track the origination of PowerHouse Industries and see where it took me. My first job was to determine who their board or directors were. No problem there was only one small issue that resulted. None of the names on the list were on the board of Saturn Futures.

There had been eight members on the PowerHouse board before the name change. After the name change there were eight members on the Saturn Futures board, none the same as before. There was no record of the sales or transfer of ownership of PowerHouse. There was just the name change and with that came a whole new board of directors. What happened to the old PowerHouse board members?

I thought I knew, but I needed to confirm it. I researched every name and found, to the person, each one was dead. How they died varied; two died from heart attacks, one a car accident, one drowned, two died in a house fire, one from cancer and the last one from hypothermia. They all died in a four-month period.

No, there was something really wrong here. None of the deaths showed any in-depth investigation as to the cause of death. They were all listed as accidental or natural. Here you have eight members of a board of directors who all die in a four-month period and no one tied it all together, come on anyway.

That told me one other thing. Whoever was behind this thing was as cold as ice. I knew then the body count was going to be huge and it wasn't going to be just contractors. Anyone and everyone could be, or was, tied to this power play would be at risk. The truth was we had already entered into a state of war.

Almost as quickly as the name of PowerHouse was changed to Saturn Futures, a whole new board of directors takes over. Because it is wholly privately owned there is no actions taken with shareholders. This whole thing stinks, that just does not happen. No, it was orchestrated, by whom I have no idea, but before I stop for the day I will know.

As I was mulling over the board issue between PowerHouse and Saturn Futures, I noted the name of the chairman of the board of PowerHouse was one Bradley R. Worthington. As I looked at the name, I realized it had not been among those members of the board of PowerHouse who had died. Bradley R. Worthington was not listed among the dead?

Now the name Bradley R. Worthington meant something. Who was he and where did he come from, if there actually was a Bradley R. Worthington? That brought me back to John Stanford. Yeah, John Stanford, he had given me the impression he was a nothing.

Sorry, now I knew he was a something and I needed to have another talk with him and it was not going to be a heart-to-heart talk. Mr. Stanford knew far more than he let on and this time I would know it all.

I decided to run a separate check on Stanford and the results set me off. That little fink had conned me and for that he was not going to survive the next encounter. He had no family and he lived in exactly the opposite direction where he had me drop him off. This time things would be different.

I had gone into this whole mess with an attitude it would be a cake walk and I would be in and out and done with it in a matter of just a few days or two weeks at the most. That was my mistake, a dumb one at that.

As it was turning out, everyone I have met and talked to in regards to Saturn Futures and Detroit Industries has lied to me from their first breath. That was going to change.

I sat there thinking about my initial contact with Stanford. He was as obvious a selection as one could get. His demeanor, the way he carried himself and his actions toward other people told me he was a nine to five person who lived just to do his job. It had been the old magician trick of distraction or misdirection. They gave me what I was looking for and I counted my blessing. Dumb!

I don't get upset often, but when I do someone's going to pay and pay big time. I needed to control my anger and think this thing out. Once it dawned on me my spotting him and kidnapping him had been orchestrated and they fed the little fink to me and I choked it all down, I was really pissed off. I hate it when someone plays me for a fool. What they didn't know was I believed in payback, one hundred percent payback.

That was it. That was my target and I needed to move now, it needed to be done as soon as possible. I knew the method I used the last time was out. This time I would have to take him hard and fast. Now he was facing Wicked and he was about to find out what being wicked really meant.

The fact was a number of people's names were registering in my mind, people I needed to talk to and get what I needed and wanted out of them, and I was good at that.

I set up at the Saturn Futures main offices where I had first seen and met Mr. Stanford. My purpose now was to do a complete reconnaissance of the building on all sides and also its subterranean layout. I knew Stanford would not appear as he had before. He knew he had conned me and he would be careful in the future. It made no difference I would find him. It was just a matter of time.

Right now, I had to work the first things first and that meant I needed to improve my reconnaissance activity concerning Saturn Futures. No detail would be left out or missed. It was to be a methodical, boring as hell, approach but one that needed to be done and done right.

As you first approach the Saturn Futures building you notice there are no windows on the first floor. It is made up of solid walls, but it is also done in a tasteful way. There are two doors, one opening on to the main street at the front of the building and one opening onto the parking lot on the west side of the building, there were no other doors. That told me I was looking at a strong-hold, a place that had a strong access and control system around it.

Next, I noted the doors, though they were glass, were made up of glass almost four inches thick. You could hit it with a car and not damage it. Besides, there were four-foot-high stanchions set into the ground in front of both doors. To gain entry one would have to have a key or have a reason for entry. I was sure there was a personnel tracking system inside as well.

Generally speaking, that was a formidable security system for the general public. However, for a contractor who needs access into a building, it was not that formidable. It just meant there would be some other method of gaining entry and I knew that was always true no matter the building or its location.

As I sat there looking at the building, I noted a small shed or hut at the far end of the parking lot away from the side entrance. That shed was about ten by ten and about nine feet high. It was made of concrete and I'm sure it was reinforced. There was one door into that shed. What was inside was anyone's guess, except I knew the general layout of most commercial buildings in the region and a shed located somewhere on the parking lot was not unusual or uncommon.

That was my best bet for gaining access to the main building. I speculate it was a utility shed and it gave one direct access to the maze of tunnels that passed under the parking area and into the subbasement of the main structure. I also noted the ventilation system was on the roof as well. I would need to follow up on that speculation, but I was sure I was right.

My research on Stanford had told me he drove a red Chevy Malibu four door. He lived in a high rise on the east side of town on the tenth floor. In scouting that place out I noted it was almost as secure as the Saturn Futures building. No matter I wasn't going to take him there anyway. No, I had other plans for him, but I still needed to penetrate the Saturn Futures building. That would have to come later, I had the time to set that aside as I dealt with Stanford. Besides I felt he had some additional information that would probably be valuable to me while I worked up the entry process for the Saturn Futures building.

It took me a week to locate and then set up on Stanford. He was a slippery little thing, but with patience and persistence I found him. This time he could not know where he was going or what was happening. This was not going to be a friendly reunion.

In my tracking John I found he loved movies. I mean this guy went at least once a week and sometimes twice, it all depended on what was showing that week. One other thing, he always went alone. Yet, there was something that was bothering me and I needed to take my time. I needed to look closer and widen my view and when I did, I saw them. That little creep had cover. I bet he was wired as well and so I set up for a hard take down.

I had learned Thursdays was his favorite day for the movies and so the following Thursday I was there and waiting. He pulled into the parking lot and drove to the farthest area away from the entrance to the theater. Sure, enough his cover pulled in half way back toward the theater from where he parked.

I had parked on the street directly in front of his car and when he left and headed into the theater, I exited my car and moved away from his car and made a wide approach to the cover car. John had already passed and gone into the theater. As he passed the cover he tapped on their driver's window. I knew he would be doing the same thing as he came back out. That's where I was going to take him.

I'm sorry but I love this kind of action. Here I had two security people sitting in this parking lot waiting for their charge to return. Their only job was to ensure he got home safe and sound. How long they had been doing this duty I had no idea, but I was sure that it had been since my first encounter with him.

No, they would be fairly easy to take down. They were bored and not paying any attention to what was going on around them. Weeks of following that little fink and just sitting there had taken its toll on their alertness. Now it was a babysitting job and the sooner he came back out and went home the sooner they could call it a day.

I moved in behind the two security men and stepped up to the passenger's side and bent over and tapped on the window. Hell, they weren't even paying any attention. I caught them by surprise and now they were going to pay for it.

Next, they assumed I was someone harmless and I had tapped on their window for assistance. Sorry guy, you blew it. As he rolled it down, I nailed him through his right eye with a .22 auto and then nailed the driver. I left both sitting there, too easy, much too easy.

About an hour and a half later I saw John come out of the theater and start walking toward the cover car. As he came up alongside of the car and tapped on the window, he stopped and bent over to look in. They hadn't responded and he reacted as any normal person would. It was then when I hit him with the stun gun. He dropped like a rag doll laying there incapable of defending himself. I then drug him over to my car and dumped him in the trunk. I had him and now he was going to find out what it's like to be wicked toward Wicked.

I headed out to my favorite location for these kinds of negotiations. I pulled into the warehouse and parked, got out and opened the trunk. He was just coming around and I hit him again and lifted him out of the trunk. The next time he came around he would be laying on the table, tied to it.

Twenty minutes later he started to come around again. I took a damp cloth and went over to him and started to wipe his face off. That helped in bringing him around. In another ten minutes he was fully awake and beginning to understand what had happened and where he was at. He was scared to death and had already wet his pants.

"Hi John, how are we doing tonight?"

He was trying to talk but nothing was coming out. That's all right I had lots of time and so I just let things develop naturally. "John, do you know who I am?"

He still was not having any luck talking but was nodding his head.

"Good I'm glad you finally figured it out. John you should have known better than to try and con me. It only works for a short time and after that your credibility with me is zero."

He was testing the bindings I had used to tie him to the table top. "Yeah John, their good bindings and they will hold firm no matter what you and I are doing."

Finally, he got his voice back and started to scream.

"John don't do that, no one can hear you anyway and besides it irritates me no end."

He finally focused on me. "What are you going to do to me?"

I looked down on him. "John, now just what do you think I'm going to do to you?

"After all, you lied your ass off the last time we met, so what do you think I would be doing with you this time. Your problem John is you have to convince me you're telling me the truth this time and frankly I doubt if you can do that."

The poor guy, no one had told him this is what was likely to happen. They had hung the poor idiot out to dry and no one but no one cared about him or what was about to happen to him. I'm sure they fed him a bunch of stuff he could regurgitate up for me and hopefully make me happy and possibly set me up for the next face-to-face.

"John, I want you to know I understand what your bosses have done to you. They have used you as a shill in this game we're playing and frankly your life is expendable. I'm really sorry about that, but there is nothing I can do about it. If I don't kill you, they will, know what I mean."

He had been looking the room over and trying to figure a way out of this. I could see the realization of the hopelessness he was feeling run across his face. I actually felt sorry for the poor dumb ass, but that's business and he got in to it at the wrong end of the show.

He then looked right at me. "Look I didn't realize until after everything had gone down just what the hell they were up to. They tricked me into this situation. I tried to leave town, but they assured me I would have protection and had nothing to worry about."

I smiled at him. "That sure as hell didn't work out now did it?"

Finally, I leaned over him and got the most serious look on my face I could. "Now you're going to tell me everything you know about Saturn Futures and how you became involved in this mess. Understand? I'm only going to give you one opportunity to let it all come out and then if I determine you're holding back or not being truthful, I'll start to take you apart one piece at a time.

John, I'm going to make you wish you were dead a dozen times over. In the end you will tell me everything you know, understand? Now if I feel you are still playing games with me, I'll cut your throat. Got me?"

He sank into the table top and just looked at me. "Now John, let's start all over with this whole mess and see if we can work our way through it and out of it, all right?"

A glimmer of hope flashed in his eyes. "Please I don't want to be in this thing and I never did. Tell me what you want and I'll give everything I can."

I suddenly had this feeling not all things were right. No, this boy was playing with me and it was time to get serious. I needed information and I needed it now and fast. He was trying to play this thing along and that meant I did not have all night. There was a time line here and I didn't know what it was. "All right John let's start with this question. You don't have a family, do you?"

"No, I've never married."

112

"The area where I dropped you off after our first visit was not the area where you really live?"

"No, I live on the east side, been there for fifteen years."

"Good, you're being honest with me, but that doesn't mean you'll continue to be. You know I've checked you out and you know I have all your personal stuff tied down, don't you?"

He was looking at me like I was some strange oddity he had never seen before. "Yes, I know, but I assure you I won't hold anything back this time."

I reached out and patted the top of his head and leaned toward him. "That my friend I can guarantee."

Now I needed to get into the company and what had taken place over these past few months. "John, how long have you been with Saturn Futures or Detroit Industries?"

"Thirteen years."

"Good, a loyal employee. All right, just what part of the company do you work in?"

"I'm an engineer and I work in the propulsion design unit."

"All right John, we're doing great. Now what happened to the original board of directors?"

He gasped a breath and started looking around in a panic. "You weren't supposed to know about that. They told me just to string you along."

"Who are they, John? Who are you talking about?"

"I can't tell you; they'll kill me if I do."

"John you don't understand, I'll kill you if you don't."

Here was a man who had agreed to do whatever, and now he was in the pot and hadn't thought his involvement over. What he didn't know was he had already told me more than he would ever realize. "Now John what happened to the prior board?"

I placed my hand on his chest and started to press down on him. "They killed them off. They made it look like accidents or natural causes, but they killed every one of them off."

Good, now he was being honest. Funny what a little mental stress and physical pressure can accomplish. "Who is Bradley R. Worthington?"

114

I pushed a little harder on his chest. "He isn't."

"What do you mean by that?"

"There is no Worthington. There is no board. It's all run out of one office located over at Detroit Industries."

"You're telling me Detroit Industries has already taken over Saturn Futures?"

"Yeah, they did that the same week the other board was killed off."

"All right you're doing fine and that explains a lot, but there are still a few things I need to know. Like why did they take Saturn Futures over?"

"I can't tell you that. Please, it could kill a lot of innocent people. You don't understand what you're asking me to do."

That was a new response and one that made me much more interested and concerned. "John, believe me when I tell you I don't want any innocent people harmed in anyway, but this information is vital if I'm going to stop Detroit Industries from doing whatever it is, they are planning. So please answer my question."

He was in agony by this time. Not because of any physical action on my part but because of the stress of what he knew and was trying not to divulge. "God, I can't do this. Please don't make me tell you."

He was right there and I needed the information, so I decided to use a little more pressure. I walked to the foot of the table and removed both his shoes and socks. I then walked over to the counter and picked up two hammers, one a sledge and the other a ballpeen and then turned and walked back to the end of the table.

He was watching me all the way and when he saw the hammers, he started to change his tune. I set the hammers down and looked right at him. "All right John I'm going to give you one more chance to be up front with me. Now why did they take over Saturn Futures?"

He wilted then, "Saturn Futures has developed a weapon system that makes all others look like child's play. The system is operational from one location and is capable of reaching any target on the face of the earth. In addition, it is capable of reaching the outposts on the Moon and on Mars."

That stunned me. If he was right then Detroit Industries was planning on a worldwide takeover and if this weapon is what he said it is then they could do it. "John,

116

you told me about another system, what about the propulsion system, what can you tell me about it?"

"That's the other project Saturn Futures has developed. What I told you about the power plants capabilities was true and has been mocked up and used. Between the two systems, whoever owns Saturn Futures owns the world."

It's not that there haven't been any huge advances in the past. In the past those kinds of advances were shared across the board to everyone. It kept everything in balance and it advanced the power base of the whole of the industrial governance system. The difference was none of those developments gave any single industry the balance of power these two projects would give.

John had spilled it all and now I knew everything and that made my life as worthless as an ice cube in a blast furnace. The question was this, what the hell good did it do me anyway? My knowing this gave me no advantage at this time, and made me the number one target for everyone out there.

I had to think and I was not going to be able to do that here. I considered letting John go, but knew he would spill it all when they picked him up and I knew they were right outside the warehouse waiting.

No John had to go and I needed to get the hell out of there. They would only wait so long and then come in after us and they planned on killing us both.

I walked around to the head of the table and patted John on the head and then put a round through his right ear. I picked up my gear and dropped down through the escape hatch and bugged out. I had a hell of a lot of thinking to do and I needed the place and time to do it in.

As I left, I activated the video system I had installed in the room. I wanted to know who would be coming after John and I. That would give me a heads up on everything and help me target my next need. What I would learn would be the one single item that would save my life.

Detroit Industries had made a huge move and they had committed everything they had on this move. On the other hand, if John had really unloaded on me, they also had the weapon of the century and the power plant to push it with. There was an even greater power fight going on behind the scenes as well.

Someone or some group was taking over both Saturn Futures and Detroit Industries and a lot of people were dying.

It was then I had the thought, what about the Board of Directors and Chairman of the Board of Detroit Industries. If there was a power play, then those people, were being targeted as well, time to go and find out.

I had this feeling in my guts again and I hate it. I knew I only had half the story at this time and the other half was going to be way beyond anything I had ever wanted to be involved in. Not only was this thing getting out of hand, it already had and big time.

The balance of power across the world was beginning to shift and it was all centering here in the Detroit Industries region. I could visualize the board rooms of all the other industries across the world at this time. They were probably running wild with fear.

No, I had that feeling I still did not know the whole story and that was the basis of my gut feeling now. I was beginning to realize I was on a one-way road and that at the end the bridge was out.

Here I was with the information I had managed to glean from the computer and from John and still I knew now it was nowhere near being complete. The problem was I had enough information to get myself killed over but not anywhere close to solving what was going on. It had already cost John his life and the lives of several others. I needed more and I needed it right now.

I knew right now I was way behind in this thing. I had been brought into it after all the real killing had been done and they needed me as a diversion. Whatever it was that had taken place, I was going to have to get into it deep and in the process kill like I have never killed before.

This was now a case of world-wide danger. If the Detroit Industries had control of those two weapons, they were way ahead on their plans to make a move against the world. It was now a case of me clearing my name and ensuring my survival and right now that was all doubtful as hell.

Chad had done me a favor by coming into the bar and warning me. I don't know if he knew what was going on, but it caused me to go after those people in the companies and then opened everything up. I knew more than anyone outside the Detroit Industries and Saturn Futures all together and that made me the biggest hazard to them. I had to die and they were going to spend every cent they had to get me.

Chapter Five

Battle Plans

    This time when I cleared the warehouse, I went the opposite direction I had gone before. A half mile down the river I had a boat stored in a garage that would take me across the river to another storage area where I had a car waiting.

    I knew there would be a dragnet out for me, so I made sure I had a car no one had ever seen me in before. I also knew I could not return to the city so I headed out into the country. I had a little man cave ten miles out that would be just right for this time, and besides that, no one knew I had it either. In this business you always maintain a hidden part of your life. A part that is always there ready for you to fall back on. This was my time and it was critical.

As I drove out to my man cave, I thought about all that had taken place so far since I had signed the contract with Detroit Industries. I had learned and collected a lot of information but still was short on what I needed. The one thing that was growing in the back of my head was the thought someone, somebody, had planned this whole thing.

Someone had orchestrated this whole situation with just one thought in mind, the time needed to complete the engine and weapons systems they had taken from Saturn Futures. It was becoming clear time was the key, it was time and there wasn't much left.

In the next few weeks, I was going to have to deal with the Detroit Industry thing and that meant I was going to have to deal with Chad as well. Knowing Chad, he would be recruiting a number of other strong and experienced contractors to assist him. What they didn't know was they were dealing with Wicked and I was as wicked as they could get or they have ever met.

It took me an hour to reach my hide away and when I got there everything was up and running. I walked over to the desk and sat down and turned the playback system on and then brought up the past hour and a half at the warehouse.

There was poor dumb John laying there with a hole through his head. I fast played through the recording until I saw the door opening and then I set it back to normal play. The door swung open and three of them moved into the room and took up positions. Good work, they did it like they should have.

They gave the all clear and in walked Chad. Sure, as hell I had that figured right, but the guy behind him really got my attention. Damn, it was Doper. How the hell did Chad get Doper to contract with him?

The last I heard, Doper hated Chad and would have killed him on sight whenever he could. No, there had to be a lot of money involved to get Doper to turn on anyone, or for that matter work with Chad.

Chad walked over to the table. "He did a number on John and I bet he got everything he wanted out of him as well."

Doper was nodding his head. "Wicked can get anything he wants out of anyone given enough time. This butt head was a push over for Wicked. Yeah, he has everything you can bet on that."

124

Doper then turned and looked directly at the camera. "Hi Den, guess you're probably a little surprised to see me here with this butt hole, but business is business and it pays really good." He then smiled. "You hang in there now and say your prayers because your ass is mine, got me."

He then pulled his gun and shot my camera off the wall.

I couldn't help but smile at the situation. If the money is big enough, I would even shoot my grandmother. Doper was doing business and he was good at it, a hell of a lot better than Chad, but not near as good as me.

With Doper involved, I knew someone was spending a lot of money just to find and take me out. That in itself was a little nerve racking, but the bottom line was why. What made me so important they had to take me out? It did not fit and I needed to figure it out before I could finalize my plan of action. So, if Doper was involved, then who else?

I sat there for a few minutes thinking over what I had learned that evening. I had been played as a patsy and now they were out to do me in. They fed me some poor dumb dude in order to get me baited and setup for the kill, but it hadn't worked. I got more than they had planned on and left little for them to work with. Now it was my time and I had a little prep work to do before I was ready to move on them.

The question that comes to one's mind is what the hell one does when dealing with a corporate giant like Detroit Industries. Well, you eat them a bite at a time, one little bite at a time. You start them bleeding and then with each bite they bleed a little more until the blood is flowing nonstop. I decided my first bite was going to be Saturn Futures.

All right it's back to the computers. Over the years I have been able to build a system within the national systems that was autonomous from all other systems. I had a number of server locations and when I entered the internet I did so from a dozen different locations at the same time. Those locations were spread out across the whole of the regions, the continental North America that is.

My system worked satellite and hard line at the same time. It took me ten years to work this system up and now it was going to pay for itself. With the level of tracking capabilities of the power brokers in the world today, you need a system that is as close to impossible to break as you can get.

Next, I sent out a number of well-placed notifications concerning the Saturn Futures issue and Detroit Industries. If all went well, within the next ten hours the phones at Detroit Industries will be coming off their hooks. I'm sure there would be special interest in regards to the weapons system that was purported to be involved, and its threat to the rest of the world.

Once that was completed, I started on my second target, that being the Saturn Futures facility downtown. I had decided to put it to the ground and the only way to really and literally do that is with explosives. It would take a special type of explosive to drop the building and it had to be military grade explosives. Not a problem, I had access to all the military grade explosives I would need. The difficulty would be getting those explosives to the building, into it and mounted.

After I had looked the building over, I determined my best bet would be through the utility shed located at the far end of the parking lot. My research had determined this shed gave access to the utility tunnel that serviced the main building, and that's all I needed to gain access to the lower levels of the building.

Third would be the targeting of the other contractors for Detroit Industries, the ones hired by Detroit Industries to take me out. I knew once a contract was let it had to be met and that meant I was to die no matter what. The only way to avoid that was to take out the contractors hired to kill me.

Once the Saturn Futures building went down Detroit Industries would be pushing the contactors to find me and carry out their contract. That was the part of the game I was depending on.

Last but not least would be the people at Detroit who made all this happen. It would be their turn to face the music, and Wicked had something special planned for them. It was a parlor game, one played by every child at one time or other and these people would have the same opportunity, what they didn't know was I owned Board Walk.

For the next week I continued my research on the Saturn facility and the means of taking it down. During this time, I was able to monitor the web concerning my notifications of the weapons systems and power plant Detroit Industries had taken over from Saturn Futures. At first there was little reaction. I had expected a more direct reaction to what I had released but after I watched for a few days I began to understand things would come about in increments.

No one was going to jump into accusations or knee jerk reactions. It would take time for them to skull things out and confirm what they had received. There was no way Detroit Industries could keep them from getting all the facts, their espionage systems were too deep and well developed. Detroit Industries had done well keeping them in the dark so far, but once they started to dig, well it was just a matter of time.

Next, I reconsidered the Saturn Futures facility. As I considered that issue, I realized destroying the building would do nothing but destroy the building. I was after the records and design work on the power plant and weapons system. Surely Detroit Industries had moved or duplicated all the design data early on. The question was where would they have taken them?

At the same time, I am dodging the other contractors who are after me. That's not a game killer but it is an irritant. In the end I will have to face them head on, but I felt that the Saturn Futures issue was the priority issue. So, it was now time to really apply myself toward that end. Detroit Industries was about to find out they had put the wrong man in the wrong position for the wrong purpose. A bunch of people were going to die as a result.

If you're going to attack something as big as Detroit Industries, you're going to need a plan and the ability to carry out that plan, that my friends is right down my alley. Oh, I can be so wicked when I apply myself and this Wicked is what they're going to get.

I knew the odds of me finding the projects were probably out of the question, but if I can't find the projects then I find the people and take them out. The problem is who do you take out? The answer is everyone and anyone associated with the projects from their board of directors to the janitor.

Yeah, you got it. I was planning on a corporate reorganization of Detroit Industries. One I'm sure they were not expecting. I think they will be rather surprised when they get their notices. Impossible, no as a matter of fact it will probably be much easier than one would think. You see what I was planning, the action I was taking no one would expect.

So, I had my battle objective done and now I needed to know who they were. When I went to their office building for my contract negotiations, I didn't meet anyone from the upper management level. No, I dealt with their attorneys and just maybe that's where I need to start now.

Yeah, that's what I want. I want the attorney, the guy who put me here. He'll make a good starting point and we'll work our way up to the king, so to speak.

After the attorney I needed to find the head over him and then the head above him all the way to their corporate board. In addition, I needed to work Chad and Doper into my plan because I would ultimately be facing off against the two of them as well. Just how and when I was not sure as yet, but they would be included.

Maybe I was taking on more than I could handle. Right now, I was after everything and everyone and just maybe that was beyond my abilities. I was trying to take everything in one bite and had forgotten to do it a small bite at a time. No, I needed to do my research and lay this thing out in detail before I try to eat it.

As I pursued my research on the board of directors, I discovered there were a dozen members on the board. Now one must realize what is provided at one web site may not match what is provided at another. I had a strange feeling the board of directors of Detroit Industries had changed and that change had been significant.

With that I started an individual search of each registered board member, guess what, every one of them except for the chairman of the board was dead. You got it, every one, and all by accident or of natural causes.

This time John had been truthful. Looks familiar doesn't it? Two boards of two different companies have been completely eliminated over the past three to four months. And that meant only one person was ruling over everything that came from Saturn Futures. Now it was all starting to make sense.

There was a power grab going on and it was targeting the whole of the world. That one person had total access to the most powerful weapons system ever created and the most powerful drive or propulsion system for the delivery of the weapon.

That meant this one person had a staff of dedicated people under him who were carrying out all of his plans, wants and needs. This was now my target, the group of people who were driving this one person's plans.

As I put my plans together, I decided I wanted to leave the head for last. I wanted to sit down with that individual, look him right square in the eyes and then put a round right between his eyes. So, as I laid my plan out, I placed his staff first. That would be followed by Chad and Doper and their crews. After them came the rest of Detroit Industries security team and then the Chairman of the Board, whoever the hell he was.

A rather aggressive plan at that, don't you think? Here I am, one individual, and I'm planning on taking out the entire organizational backbone of Detroit Industries. Again, let me emphasis something here. In the normal world, organizations compete and live under stringent rules and guidelines. In my world, that does not exist. There are no rules. There are no guidelines. It's a dog-eat-dog existence and the top dog is the one who is the most brutal and aggressive.

What I needed now was time, the time to set things up and prepare for my assault on this monster. I had been working, fighting, and dodging for the past two month and now it was time to get ready. I sat there looking at the calendar and decided to give me one month to the day for my plan to be initiated. That would be the third month anniversary of my contract signing, such a wicked idea.

Every good plan has any number of false actions designed to draw the attention and activity of the target organization away from your real action plan. This would be no different. It was then I realized my first consideration of attacking the Saturn Futures building was actually the perfect thing to do. Damn that was perfect. Take the entire facility out and then while they're working on that issue, I hit their staff team.

Now, who the hell is their staff team? Back to the computer and to Detroit Industries. As I looked for the upper management, I found the directory for that group. As I studied the files, I could determine all those who were staff members to the other past board members and leave them out of this. That left the Chairman and his staff, and there it was right down to my friend who put the contract together and signed off with me.

As I scanned the names and their office locations, I was surprised to find the entire staff was located in the Saturn Futures building. That caused me to stop and start to rethink this whole mess. Why would they move all those staff members over to that building when the Detroit Industries building was a far superior fortress than the Saturn building?

Beautiful, just damn beautiful, the Chairman had set his staff up as a shield for him. They got hit and it gave him the time he would need to prepare or react. Good move, but not good enough. That only meant I was going to have to coordinate my actions a little tighter. What they didn't know was I could do it and would.

All I had to do was work the plan so in the end I was standing at the door to the Chairmen's office for our final board meeting. So, here's how it would go down.

I would need to arm the Saturn building from the basement to the penthouse. My studies of the place showed the central core of the building was occupied by stairways and elevator shafts, which was normal for a building this size and height. The building itself was five stories high.

The upper two floors were designated management occupation and the top floor was the Chairman and Board of Directors. My primary target would be those two floors and the bulk of my explosives would be dedicated there. Yes, I planned on dropping the whole of the structure but I wanted to ensure those two floors were completely destroyed.

As I sat there looking at the plan, I had an idea cross my mind. What if the Chairman was not in the Saturn building? In fact, I would bet my life he was not. That sneaky little asshole, he was still in the Detroit Industries building and he has hung his staff out to dry. All right, I have the staff nailed down and I know where the Chairman will be, but I also had to deal with Chad and Doper.

I didn't want to meet them in either of the two company buildings. That gave them too great an advantage so I needed to get them to where I wanted to fight. I needed them on my ground and not theirs. And that brings up the warehouse.

Yeah, that was the place I would need to draw them to the warehouse, and then settle our differences there. I expected a five-man team plus Doper. Chad would coordinate and that meant he would stay at the main entrance.

He would send in two snipers into elevated positions and then send in two flushers. I was sure Doper would be a rover and that made matters most difficult.

Timing, that would be the key to everything. I had to set up the timing so when the Saturn building went, I already had the hit team on me and heading to or into the warehouse. I had to leave the location of the Chairman in a flux and would need to find and drive him to ground after I finished with the hit team.

I knew I was working a hell of a lot into that time frame, and if any one of the actions failed to develop at the projected time it could throw everything off. I normally don't set things up this tight, but I was pressed for time and I had to get this thing moving. I felt it was a risk worth taking and decided to leave it at that.

As I sat there looking over the logistics the thought came to me, if I could identify the Chairman's car or cars, I could mark them and at least have an idea as to where they were at any given time. I needed to spend some time scouting the Detroit Industries building and the traffic coming in and out of it. That became my next priority and I set out to do just that.

Coordination was the key to this whole thing. I needed to set this thing up so the dropping of the Saturn Futures building and the faceoff with Chad, his team and Doper were timed right. I wanted the Chairman to know he had been hit hard and his contractors were out as well.

Sometimes the best way to hide is to sit down in plain sight and that's just what I did. I drove downtown and parked in the nearest parking garage and walked over to the Detroit Industries building. As I walked around the perimeter of the building, I noted the several entrances and garage entrances around the building.

Finally, I came across one entrance that was all by itself and facing the street. This entrance was large and clearly a garage door, but this one was solid, by that I mean armored, and appeared to be secure. That was the Chairman's private entry into the building.

I looked around at the buildings across the street from that entrance and spotted an elevated patio or garden area on the second floor of the building across from the garage entrance. I crossed the street and entered the building and walked up to the second floor. It was more than a patio or park it was a food court. By this time, it was eleven thirty and lunch was coming, a perfect time to watch for any activity.

I stopped at a stand and got a sandwich and a coffee and walked over to the edge of the patio and took a seat. The next few hours would be spent reading a book and writing notes. I wanted to appear to be a person working on a project and not interested in anyone around or near him. On the other hand, I needed to be aware of who was around me and may be approaching me.

The table I selected was a square two chair table sitting right up against the wall and overlooking the street below. Across from me was the armored garage door, I was in a perfect position to observe any vehicle leaving or entering the building. At the same time, I was in the perfect position to watch for anyone approaching my table from the food court area.

At about ten minutes after twelve the garage door opened and a large black Cadillac pulled out of the garage and onto the street. I focused in on the license plate and wrote it down. Because the windows were darkened, I was not able to see who was in the car, but I had a license number and that was a start.

Two hours later the same Cad came back and the gate opened and it entered. That was it and I headed out of the area and back to my office. I sat down at the computer and started a search on the Cad. That resulted in little information other than being registered to the Detroit Industries.

The best I could do was to assume the Cad was the Chairman's vehicle. The truth was it could have been anyone in that Cad and I could have spent the better part of the day sitting there in the food court and getting the license plate number of a car that meant nothing.

I sat there looking at the screen and thinking. There was something odd going on here. So far, I have been able to identify the board of directors and the Chairman's immediate staff, but the Chairman remains a mystery. I ran a check on several other industrial giants and found the Chairman of the Boards readily available and identifiable. Damn, there was something out of place here.

There was that tick again, a small touch in the mind telling me something is really out of balance. Something was not right and I couldn't see it. I have never had this much trouble getting information on anyone before but here I had been stumped. It was like getting hit across the forehead with a baseball bat. I needed to think.

Clearly there's been a successful move by the Detroit Industries to take over Saturn Futures and the two major projects I have been able to identify. But trying to identify the Chairman of the Board has been impossible so far.

I then had a thought. I would do a search on the historical background of the board of directors and try to set up a lineage as to who has served on the company boards of both companies.

It took me five hours to come up with a listing of those who had served on the board and also identified the Chairman during all that time as well. It appeared things started to change about nine years ago. At the time a Mr. Mannington was elected Chairman of the board of Detroit Industries and was clearly working the position for the next seven years.

Then another change took place about two years ago. Mr. Mannington's activity fell off abruptly at the time. He was still there, but his name stopped appearing on documents and corporate letter heads. At the 18 months mark Mr. Mannington disappeared altogether and a new Chairman of the Board, a Mr. Worthington appeared. Bradley R. Worthington, the same name for the Chairman of the Board at Saturn Futures.

A quick check on when that name appeared at Saturn Futures showed he became the Chairman eight months ago and every member of both boards of the two companies have all died, one hundred percent.

It was becoming quite clear the key to everything I am dealing with is this Mr. Bradley R. Worthington and I needed to track him down. Yet, another name came up at this time, one that seemed to sit in the background. That names' position in relationship to the board and Chairman was odd. This person's name was Costello.

I could find nothing on him prior to the takeover by Worthington. The name just popped up and has remained there. One could think of it as a typo except it appears three times and, in each situation, it was a critical location in the reforming of the two boards.

Good job, now I was starting to get some things done. With the information on the Chairman, I knew the entire upper management levels of both companies had been wiped out to the last person with one or maybe two exceptions, survivor Bradley R. Worthington and then this Costello person.

Still there was something wrong. I could feel it. It was not that simple. A lot of energy and expense has gone into the removal of both those boards and then the selection of the new board over both companies. What really got me was that it was all done in that time frame and yet they were able to shield the real identity of Mr. Worthington and the removal of Mr. Mannington.

It then hit me, with the Saturn Futures Board it had been a rather simple process to select and appoint a new board. It was an in-house holding company and therefore it did not need any input from any shareholders.

But Detroit Industries was a public holding company and it had shareholders, so how the hell did they get the board change to move in so fast and so smoothly without an issue with the shareholders. That one had me stumped.

Things were starting to irritate me all to hell and when my level of irritation goes up my level of stubbornness goes off the chart. No, I would skull this thing out, and when I did, I would take the appropriate steps in dealing with this mess.

One thing I knew at this point, I had developed a number of leads and opened the door to all that had been going on in the Detroit Industries building these past several months. The information was coming grudgingly, but it was coming one small piece at a time.

I still had a number of holes in my evidence list but they were being filled in slowly, much too slowly at that. Never-the-less a picture was developing and so far, what I could see of it I didn't like. I was making progress and the more I moved ahead the better my overall position in this chess game became.

Chess game, yeah, this was a chess game and right now my king was in a bad way. My queen was running for her life and the rest of the board was spread all over hell and creation. I knew something had to start happening soon or my time would clearly go down the tube and they would get what they wanted, world domination.

Hell, I didn't care about world domination, what I cared about right now is me, my life, living another week or month or two. Besides, I was just plain pissed off. I'm running from God only knows how many contractors, no one can tell me the truth and now we have two inventions that could destroy the world. How the hell could it get any worse.

Chapter Six

Corporate Take Over

So far, I had determined the full membership of two boards of directors and the Chairman of one of those boards had all been eliminated. Don't think for a minute they all died by accident or natural causes in that same time frame. No, they were escorted to the afterlife and there was no doubt about it, all of them except for the Chairman of the Board at Detroit Industries.

That was easy to discern, the problem comes with the identity of the Detroit Industries Chairman. I then had an idea and went back to the computer. This time I went looking for the Board of Directors for Detroit

Industries back ten years to try and see if there was a tie in or something that stood out.

There it was, his name popped out just like all the other board members in any company across the world, Bradley R. Worthington. The sickness washed over me as I sat there looking at that name. No, that was impossible but there it was the same person who was the head of the Saturn Futures. His name was in the board member's position before the Saturn Futures even came on the scene.

I went back to Saturn Futures and there it was, Bradley R. Worthington, one of the founding members of Saturn Futures. A direct tie between the two companies and it had always been there. But when did the change take place?

I knew it was within the last eight months. In that time frame Mannington and the members of both boards had been eliminated and one figure was now in charge over both companies. The question now was whether it was Mr. Worthington or someone else, that someone being Costello.

I picked the phone up and made the call. When the receptionist answered I asked for Paul Bigamy. There was a pause and then she answered. "One moment please."

The line went quiet and then a male voice came on the line. "This is Mr. Bigamy."

"Yes, Paul this is Denton Wicked, I need to talk to you."

It was quiet as a tomb on the other end of the line. "Mr. Wicked, I don't know that we can do that."

I had expected that reaction. "Paul we either do it or your ass is going to be mine and it will be permanent."

He knew full well who he was talking to and you could hear the strain enter his voice. "Look Mr. Wicked there is nothing I can say or do for you. We had a contract and you failed on it."

That was normal. "No Paul I have not failed on it; I have only begun to carry it out. Now you and I can end this thing here and now or we can get together and you can answer a few questions for me."

His voice changed to that of a man who considered the person he was talking to not to be on the same level as he was. It was aloof and self-assured. "Mr. Wicked I'm sorry but that's not going to happen. I don't know or understand what you thought you could gain by calling me like this, but you've gained nothing, you sir, are nobody and you're about to be eliminated. Do you understand?"

Damn he was sure of himself, but he failed to understand I got what I wanted and now it was my move. He was at work at the Detroit Industries building and my knowing where he was set him up for a visitor, he will wish he'd never met.

"Paul, listen to me, don't play that game with me. You know why I'm calling and you also have the answers for me so I would suggest you make the arrangements for us to come together and address these issues."

"Screw you." And he hung up.

A check of the computer and a quick check of the clock and I was off heading for the Detroit Industries building parking lot exit. It was a forty-minute drive to that location and as I turned the corner I pulled up across the street from where the parking lot exit was. I stopped in front of a news stand directly across from the exit. It took me five minutes to get my paper and just as I opened the main section I looked over and saw Paul's car coming out of the lot. It turned right and headed west.

I pulled in behind him and back three cars and maintained my position in relationship to his. By my side I had my .40 and a stun gun. The .40 was for the driver security officer, and the stun gun was for Paul. As we moved out and away from the city's central district the traffic started to thin and I dropped back further, giving them all the room in the world. In addition, I was looking for any other security units that may be working Paul. There were none.

Ten minutes later they pulled into a shopping mall and the car pulled up in front of a hair dressers business and Paul exited and entered the business. The driver then pulled away and drove around and found a place to park toward the back of the lot where he could see the front entrance of the business and watch for Paul to come out.

I parked three rows back from the car and driver and exited my car and walked the distance to the car and its driver. As I approached the car, I brought the .40 up and put a round right into his left ear. As he fell over, I opened the door and reached in pushing the body on over and onto the passenger's seat and then down onto the floor. I then got in the driver's seat and waited.

It was a full forty-five minutes later when I saw Paul come out the front door of the business. I sat there a few seconds until he looked over toward the car and waved me toward him. I started the car and drove around and up to where he was standing. He got in the back door and closed the door and looked up at me. I gave him a smile and then hit him with the stun gun and out he went. I wanted so much just to shoot the little fart right then and there but managed to control myself. I needed the information and that would keep him alive for a few more hours.

A half hour later I had finished laying him on the table and tying him down when he started to come around. "Good you're waking up. You feel alright Paul?"

He looked around and then down at the straps holding him to the table and then looked up at me. "What the hell is going on here?"

"Paul, relax and I'll fill you in on everything. Now you need to listen to me carefully because your stinking little life is going to depend on it. Hear me?"

The magnitude of his situation was just starting to settle in as I finished talking. I could see the blood draining out of his face as he tried to test the strength of the straps holding him. "You're a damn fool if you think you're going to get away with this."

Why did everyone take the attitude I couldn't do whatever it was I was doing. Hell, all they had to do is look at the position they were in and they would know I could. "Paul I would save my breath at this time because you and I have a lot to discuss and a short time to discuss it in. I'm going to be asking you a number of simple questions and you my friend are going to give me the answers. Understand?"

He was still struggling with the straps when my first blow hit him in the right kidney area. What blood still in his face left it along with his breath. I leaned over him, looking him straight in the eyes. "Now that I have your attention, I need to know a few things, the first of which was why you, your boss, your supervisor, and anyone else found it necessary to set me up the way you did?"

He was still trying to catch his breath. "You're crazy as hell. What are you trying to do anyway, get yourself killed?"

Damn, I couldn't believe these people. That was the dumbest thing anyone laying on a table in front of me had ever said. Things that stupid drive me nuts and I wanted to beat the shit out of him and forget about any information.

I stepped back, looked down at him and turned to walk away and then came around with my second punch hitting him in the same kidney area as the first blow. The breath went out of him along with a long hard scream. "I'll not repeat the question. Now answer it."

I slowly walked around to the other side of the table watching him and waiting for an answer. This was going to be a tough one, but I've handled tougher. As I approached the other side, I hit him on that side right in the kidney again.

This time he lost control and wet himself. "Damn those hurt and they'll get much worse as I continue hitting you there. You need to know after a few more blows you'll start to piss blood and in time those blows will damage the kidneys and then you'll be in serious trouble. Now answer the question."

I gave him the time needed to regain his composure and he finally signaled with his hands he was ready. I looked down at him. "Now answer the question."

His spittle hit me in the left cheek and I reached up and wiped it off. "Paul that was the dumbest thing I have seen anyone do in a long time." As I talked to him, I reached down and took his left hand and calmly broke his little finger and then I moved over and broke the ring finger and then the middle finger.

I set his hand down and patted him on the face and moved back around to the other side of the table. The fourth blow hit dead center on the kidney.

He started screaming and tearing at his straps. He was in total pain and it was going to get worse in short order. "Now Paul for the fourth time, answer the question and do it now."

"All right, all right I'll tell you. You were the obvious one because of your reputation. We needed as much action as we could get while making our final organizational adjustments. We knew you would not go down easy and so we got two of the best we could find to take you out. They're not done yet and you're still going to die."

I smiled at him and leaned back over him and put my hand over his mouth. "Good you're doing fine. Now why was it necessary to kill those two boards off?"

He looked at me and shrugged his shoulders. "We need total control and with two boards to deal with there were just too many opinions and possible sources of opposition. This was the most expeditious means of taking care of the problem."

That sounded reasonable, but maybe just maybe it was a little over kill. "All right, you're doing great. Now who the hell is Bradley R. Worthington?"

A look of surprise flashed across his face when I asked that question. He seemed to quiet. "I really don't know. I have never met the man and I don't know anyone who has."

He lay there looking at me and saw the shadow of disbelief move across my face.

"No please that's the truth. I have never met him or talked to him. Any contact I've had with him has been through my boss Marsha Wilson, she's the head of the legal department."

That could be reasonable and so I decided to drop it for now. "All right Paul I believe you. Now tell me about the Saturn Futures projects. Where are they located and how far along are, they?"

"Aww man you're going to get me killed you know that?"

"Yeah, Paul that is probably true, but that's not my problem what I need now is the information I just asked you about. Now please consider your situation and tell me what I want to know. He just laid there looking at me.

I waited for a minute or two and then continued. "Paul do you know my name?"

He looked at me and nodded his head.

I smiled at him and then ran my hand over his left arm. "Paul my name is Wicked and I'm here to tell you I am capable of living up to that name. What I've done to you so far is nothing. Believe me when I tell you when I start to flay your feet and legs you will wish to God you had talked sooner. Know what I mean?"

I walked over to the counter and opened the drawer and started pulling out the flay knives and cutting board. I heard it coming from deep down inside of him. It was a growl of sorts, but still a growl. There was all the pain and fear held deep inside a man coming out all at the same time.

He lost control of everything this time, and started to cry. He then started to beg.

156

"Please don't do this. I'll tell you everything you want to know to the best of my ability. I don't know it all. I'm only privileged to a certain level and then that's it."

I kept setting things out. "The weapons system is still in the Saturn building. It's about ninety percent complete now but the preliminary tests indicate it's going to be a lot more potent than we first thought. Nothing can stand against it.

"The propulsion system is complete and being prepared for mass production. That system is at the Dearborn plant and is already in production." He was scared almost to death and I knew I could get anything I wanted out of him.

I set the knives down. "What's the time schedule?"

"They plan on producing two thousand propulsion units in three weeks starting at five O'clock in the evening three days ago, the weapons system is still a month out."

"Who's their first target?"

"Dallas and the Oil Industry."

"And after that?"

"They are going for the railroads and trucking industries. After that it will be the shipping and airlines."

"What is their total control timeline set for?"

"In three months, they plan on controlling eighty percent of the world's industry and the other twenty percent within a year after that."

I stood there looking at him. The guy was spilling everything he knew and then some. "All right I have one last question. Is there anything you can give me on this Worthington person?"

He was shaking his head and then stopped and a look of surprise came across his face. "Worthington's a woman."

"Bullshit, you're trying my patience again." I really didn't believe him and my temper was starting to kick up again.

"No really Worthington is a woman. I remember Marsha talking about some of the directives that had come down, and she referred to the Chairman as she and her. No, I'm telling you the Chairman is a woman."

I stood there weighing what information I had gotten from Paul and then concluded I had everything I needed. I walked over to him and pulled my .40 and pushed the barrel against his chest and pulled the trigger. He didn't make a sound but had a wild look of total fear tear across his face. He then went limp and his face collapsed into quietness. I pulled him off the table and drug him to the side door and dumped his body into the river. I went to his car and drove back to the mall and got my car and went back to my office.

For the next two weeks I spent each night carrying a load of high explosives to the underground in the downtown area and loading the Saturn building for destruction. The bulk went to the foundation of the structure and the rest were set up as kickers to help the collapse along once it started. The real difficult part was the hiding of the explosives as I placed them. I had to find locations where the force of the explosions could be contained and cause the greatest damage. When I was done, I had no doubt she would go all the way to the ground.

When I was done, I concentrated on tracking Worthington so she would be in the Detroit Industries building when I put the assault into action. Unfortunately, there was more guess work involved in that project than good planning.

What I did find out was she never missed a day on the job, never, and so I could depend on her being there during the normal business hours. So, I set things up for the time I wanted everything to go. That was set for nine that evening. She would be there; I was sure of that. Once she heard of the Saturn Futures building going down, she would respond and I would find her in her office in the Detroit Industries building.

Yeah, you're thinking one man couldn't do that. One man couldn't load a building the size of the Saturn Futures building with enough explosives to bring it down. Don't worry about it. When it goes off it will take the building down. The military explosives of today are potent and exceptional in their destructive capabilities. No, it will come down, trust me.

That day finally came and I needed to get Chad and his crew to the warehouse. I made the call and he answered on the first ring. "Chad, Wicked here. Don't say a word. I'll be at the warehouse on River Port Drive tomorrow night at nine o'clock. If you want a crack at me, be there, otherwise you're out of this game." When I hung up, I could hear him trying to interject and I let it pass.

At his end of the call Chad was trying to muscle in on Wicked but wasn't making any headway. After Wicked hung up he threw

160

the phone against the wall. "I'll have his spleen for that."

Things were now set and I needed to get to the Saturn building by eight in order to set the charges. I was targeting nine o'clock for everything to come together and then go off and hopefully I would have Chad nailed down and give him the opportunity to hear the building go before I ended things. Once I was done with Chad, I would give the Chairman an hour to get to the Detroit Industries building and then I would be going for him or her, whichever.

I expected the Saturn building to drop all the way into the basement area. The responding emergency units would be tied up with that major collapse leaving me to my business in the Detroit Industries building.

I started to review my scouting missions to the Detroit Industries building. I had the main communications lines tapped and would set those charges remotely when I got to the building. If all went well, I would have the top three floors isolated when I started my assault.

At six I loaded up my gear and dropped several more clips of .40 rounds into my back pack and mounted my .40 to my belt. I got in the car and headed downtown to set the Saturn building charges at eight.

When I had made my initial entry into the underground at the Saturn building, I had gone through the utility shed at the end of the parking lot at the building. Once into the underground I worked out a whole new approach to the location through the cities underground systems. Now I could park in a safe zone and approach the building without being observed.

That task was completed as planned and I headed for the warehouse. If I failed at the warehouse then I had nothing to be worried about, I would be out of the game. I needed to complete this meeting by nine-thirty so I could be back at the Detroit Industries building by ten. It was a tight schedule but one I could meet if everything fell into place.

That was the way it all had gone down up till my business with Chad and his boys here at the warehouse. I was prepared to finish Chad off and head for Detroit Industries. Until now it had all gone well and I felt I was on top of everything.

Yeah, I was wounded and a little worn out but other than that I was high on adrenaline and ready to take on the Detroit Building back down town.

I stood there looking down at Chad as he slowly lifted his head looking up at me. Our eyes met and he started to speak. "Damn Wicked you're good. I never thought anyone could take Doper out like that."

He sank back to the ground and I stood over him looking down. I couldn't help but love the guy, we had been buddies for years, but this time the money was just too much and he went for it. "Sorry Chad, I didn't want us to end up on the wrong side from one another, but that's the way it goes."

He raised his left hand again and smiled. "Hey, it's all right. We all make our choices and I chose to make a run on you and I lost. You're too good and besides you're wicked as hell. Hang in, there Den and put a round through that bitch for me."

He settled back and went quiet. I walked over to the box on the wall, opened it and set the remote switch, turned and headed for the escape door. Ten minutes later I was across the field on the dike watching the cars pull up. I checked my watch and then pushed the button and headed for my car.

Chad had said bitch, so he knew who Worthington was, and she was a woman. That would prove to be worth more than anything I could imagine. Just then I heard the rumble and crack of explosions going off toward town. As I looked that way, I could see the fireball rising above the buildings. The Saturn building had gone up. I had an hour to get to the Detroit Industries building and prepare my entry.

Chapter Seven

Attack on Detroit

As I came in on the downtown area, I parked a couple of blocks away from the Detroit Industries building and started to walk to the area. There were a lot of people milling around and talking to each other about what had happened. I was able to hear the Saturn building had blown up and collapsed in on itself. There had been a number of people in the upper floors involved in a meeting when the place went. There appeared to be no survivors.

I continued on to the Detroit Industries building area. Most of the streets were cordoned off but access to the Detroit building was not restricted. People were milling around the building and up on the upper entrance portico so they got a better look at the Saturn building area.

I started to look around for Detroit Industries building security personnel and finally spotted them. Most were standing in the lobby area looking out toward the Saturn disaster. I moved back around to the other side of the building where there was a side door into the lobby area. It was locked but that was not my point of entry. I knew when I entered the garden area along that side of the building there was a utility door that could be opened from the inside out. It was well secluded from the rest of the garden, giving me time to work it open.

I placed one pry bar at the bottom of the door under the door and between it and the threshold. I then stepped on the pry bar and jammed the second bar into the space between the striker plate and receiver plate of the door and gave it a hard push. The combined pressure sprung the door and it opened and I slipped in taking both pry bars with me.

I found myself in the maintenance room for the main floor. This room gave access to all the electrical systems for the building including the elevators. I set my timed charges for the elevators and then located and dismantled the communications systems for the building. I then waited to see if anything happened. It was quiet as I moved out of the maintenance room and over to the stairwell door. After entering the stairwell, I placed a termite charge in the locking mechanism for the door and set it off. That welded the lock shut and dismantled the door.

I moved to the second-floor entrance for the lobby and took the elevator to the floor just below the top management level floor. When I got there, I exited the elevator and entered the stairwell and moved up to the first management floor. I entered the floor and scouted it out, finding no one present. I continued up to the second management floor and did the same there.

It was now time to go up to the top floor. That whole floor was for the Chairman of the Board and his or her staff. If everything worked right, I would find my target there.

As I exited the stairwell, I spotted the reception desk and the young lady sitting behind it. I walked up to her as she looked up at me. I had my .40 leveled on her and she sat there saying nothing and not moving. When I got to her desk I leaned over. "I need to see the Chairman and I need to see him now, understand?"

She was nodding her head. "Yes, sir he's in. but I don't know if he will see you. Do you want me to call and ask?"

I didn't know if she was just scared or was so well trained the sight of a gun being pointed at her didn't bother her in the least bit. That should have told me something. I smiled at her. "No, I think we'll just go in and surprise him."

I walked around the desk and took hold of her arm and lifted her out from behind the desk and walked her toward the door to the inner offices. The sign on the door said Chairman. I stopped and leaned down to her ear. "Now listen to me and hear me, we will go through this door and you will be right in front of me. Any fast moves by anyone in this office and you're the first one dead."

She was nodding her head as I reached out and turned the nob. I pushed the door open and pushed her through in front of me. There were two men sitting in chairs to our right. The rest of the office was empty. I then asked her. "Are there any side rooms someone could be in?"

She shook her head no and I pushed on into the room. As the door closed, I looked at the two men. "Which of you is the Chairman of Detroit Industries?"

Neither one said a word or made a move. I felt the woman move slightly and then one of the men stood. "Why I'm the Chairman of Detroit Industries, what's going on here?"

I leaned closer to the woman and put my lips right by her right ear and then turned my gun on the standing man and pulled the trigger. "That's not the Chairman. Do you want to try that again?"

"OK, I'm the Chairman who the hell are you anyway?"

I swung my .40 around and knocked the other man down and then spun her around. "I'm the guy you hired to deal with the Saturn Futures issue. I'm also the guy you hired others to hunt down and kill as a means of hanging the killing of two boards of directors on me and then the taking of the Saturn Futures. Now do you know who I am?"

I felt her stiffen up as she heard my words. I also know you're the Chairman of the Board and you are responsible for the killing of the members of both the Board of

169

Directors for Saturn Futures and Detroit Industries. Your name is Bradley R. Worthington. That one threw me I had never met a woman named Bradley. What does the R. stand for?"

She looked up at me. "RaAnn."

She then pulled away from me and I let her go. She walked over to the windows looking out toward the Saturn building and then turned back to me. "You think you've stopped me, don't you?"

I looked around and shrugged my shoulders. "It sure as hell looks like it." There was that same old feeling again, there was something wrong here and I was standing right in the middle of it.

She continued to smile. "You really don't know what you've got yourself into, do you? You don't have the slightest idea as to what is going on and who I really am? And the sad part about it is you're going to die here tonight and no one will ever know anything about this other than some crazy stupid man tried to kill off these two companies."

She sat down at the desk and sat back in her chair. "I've been dealing with idiots like you all my life, and when it comes down to the real issues you never know anything and when you die you die wondering just what the hell happened." She shifted in her seat and then continued. "I've got nothing but contempt for your kind. You stir things up and make one hell of a mess and then you're gone and it's everything back the way it was. You're a waste of time and effort.

"In five minutes, the whole of my security unit will be up here. Your best bet is to use that gun on yourself and do it now. If you kill me you've accomplished nothing, nothing at all."

I smiled at her and raised my .40 at her and then panned over to the window behind her and fired four rounds through it. I walked around the desk, grabbed her and cuffed her hands behind her and then drug her over to the window. I pulled my jacket off and grabbed her by the waist and stepped out the window and pushed off.

She started to scream the minute I stepped through the window. I released the drone chute as we cleared the window and the parachute deployed five seconds later. She turned her head and looked at me. "You'll never make it." There was a degree of panic in her voice.

"Yeah, I will but you won't."

At then I let go of her and watched as she dropped away from me. She kept her eyes on me as she fell away and then slipped out of sight. She was a tough one and when faced with death she was as cold as ice. I don't know there just seemed to be something wrong with this whole thing. By all the work I had done I knew Worthington was a woman, but which woman was she. A cold chill washed over me; I killed the wrong woman.

As I worked my way to the ground, I felt the sharp pain of knowing I had screwed up. I didn't know who that was and I didn't know who the chairwoman was and it was my fault. I got too aggressive and tried to run this thing with the information I had. Granted I was having one hell of a time getting the information I needed, but still I moved too soon and someone else paid for the chairwoman. I hate it when I get beat that way. I could just see her sitting someplace laughing at me and shrugging the death of that woman, whoever she was, off as a simple sacrifice.

This game wasn't over yet, not by a long shot. I had given Detroit Industries a severe beating, but it was not going to be enough. The Chairwoman still lived and I still had no idea who she was or where she was. This one was far more in control and intelligent than I had given her credit for. It was the age-old adage, not to take your opponent lightly.

Yeah, I had successfully made my escape from the Detroit Industries building and returned to the office and was now thinking this thing over. All right, big deal, so what, it was obvious I had missed something. So far that individual had played a good chess game with me, in fact she was beating my butt for me.

The first thing I needed to do was, after getting back to my hideout, to sit down and think this thing over. If everything had gone the way I had hoped I knew the weapons system had been wiped out with the blowing up of the Saturn building. That left the Dearborn facility where the power plant was being developed and produced. It then struck me she was there and had been all along.

The second thing to come to my mind was those working for the Chairwoman were far more dedicated to her than I had anticipated. That probably meant Paul Bigamy and John Stanford had not told me the whole story or had lied about everything from the beginning. All right there was one other person I needed to locate now and have a heart to heart with, and that was Marsha Wilson.

Marsha Wilson, hell she could be anywhere if she is still alive. She's the only name I have tied into everything. It then hit me. I broke out in a cold sweat when the thought hit me, was the one I dropped this Marsha Wilson?

Damn I hated even the idea I had been suckered again. If it was true, I had killed the last connection I knew of to the Chairwoman. I needed to find out, and I needed to, first thing in the morning. If that was Marsha Wilson then I was in trouble and the only direction I had left was the Dearborn plant.

There was one other issue, and it was whether anyone else was looking for me. I would bet everything I own not only is someone looking for me, but everyone in the whole of the Detroit Industries was probably looking for me, and it was not to talk.

I had just won a battle but was clearly losing the war. I had managed to knock out every access point I knew of to the Chairwoman and now I was in a real guessing game. On top of that I was now running blind with a target on my back. Hell, yes, she had more contractors coming at me, she would be a fool not to.

The following morning, I turned on the television and started to watch the news. The top story was the Saturn building followed closely by the Detroit Industries building invasion at the same time last night. It was toward the end of the news a final footnote was presented and was the finding of a handcuffed woman in the street less than two blocks away from the Detroit Industries building. She was identified as Marsha Wilson and her death was being investigated as a homicide.

Damn, the last name I had in relationship to everything that had happened these past three months, was now dead as well. Talk about a dead end. It was literally a dead end and everyone I knew of who could have had additional information on this thing was dead. It was thinking time now and I had better come up with something.

Now wait a minute. The company did not run itself. It was made up of thousands of people all working in assigned areas and carrying out assigned duties. When you consider the fact the top three stories of the Detroit Industries building were dedicated to corporate management or the elite in the business world, then there were others. My job was to find them and then identify them. The Chairwoman was still out there and I still needed to find her, or him, or whomever.

The Board of Directors were now gone, they had died in the Saturn Futures building explosion. But it still left Worthington and the other person, this Mr. Costello. Mr. Costello? Could it be he was the real Chairman and Worthington was just a cover, a target to draw me away from Costello?

My next concern was the fact I took out the better part of their security and hit teams at the old warehouse. I have no doubt they will bring in more contractors and I will be on a hot list to find and eliminate. That meant I would need to pay close attention to everything and everyone. The game was now total war and I was standing target dead center.

Now it was time to shift gears, I would have to kill without hesitation and leave nothing to chance. My first job was to track down and locate all other contractors currently available. That's not too difficult a task because when contractors are available, they let the power brokers of the industrial world know they are available.

The other side of the story is that many industries keep contractors on a contingency contract so they don't have to go looking when they need one. That would narrow my search down and reduce my time schedule. I knew most contractors never worked on a contingency contract. They took each contract as it came up, and when not under contract they either relaxed or worked freelance. Yet there were a few who accepted and desired contingency contracts. Those were the ones I was looking for.

The only other concern would be the possibility the Chairwoman brought in a contractor or contractors from outside. That is someone from somewhere else in the world, and it was clearly possible. If that happened then I was in real trouble, there was no way to determine who that person would be or where he or she came from. All right that was a good possibility, but I needed to stay with the obvious and that was the location of any local contractors.

I finished the research in three hours and found there were five contractors who were listing themselves available at this time. As I tried to determine their location, I found only two, the other three were off the grid and could only mean one thing.

I knew all three of these people and each one was cold as ice. Two were what I would call mediocre contractors. They worked fast and failed to work the details; in other words, they were sloppy. They would be relatively easy to track down. The third one though, was skilled and deadly, it was Tangle.

Cheater and Bouncer would come running right at me, and if I paid attention, they would telegraph their presence. These two would actually be running interference for Tangle. They wouldn't know it but he would use them anyway he could.

As I saw things right now the game was between Tangle and me. The other two would be used as cover. We would both, work to keep those two between us until the situation and location was right for our face to face. Both of the other contractors were expendable at this point, but I still had to be careful. More than once a lower-level contractor has taken a lucky shot and scored a hit.

Cheater was young, good looking and deadly. With a little discipline he could be at the top of the heap, but his age simply would not let him do that. He was overly confident in his abilities and with the average target he had little or no problem, but when facing an experienced contractor, it was a different game. No, Cheater would come right at me, probably in a crowd in hopes I would hold back because of the presence of the innocent. Sorry, Wicked doesn't work that way.

Bouncer was a little more of a problem or challenge. He was big and powerful and could kill you in seconds with his bare hands. He would try to take me by surprise from behind and discretely. No upfront attack for him. He wanted it in the dark and out of sight of anyone else. He loved the one on one and the ability to take his time and watch his victim succumb in his hands. Two years ago, I had the chance to take Bouncer out, but I decided not to at the time, now I wish I had.

Then there was Tangle, he was something altogether different and that made him dangerous. He has been around for a long time and he knows more ways to kill you than there are hairs on a dog. No, I would have to go after Tangle. No waiting for him or walking into his choice of location. I would need to find him, track him and kill him without his having any chance to react or take me head on. The only difficult thing about Tangle was he and I had lived a lifetime together.

The only other possible problem that could come out of this thing would be if they teamed up and came at me as a unit. That was possible, but with Tangle in the game, probably not probable. From a team perspective I could see Cheater and Bouncer teaming up, but not Tangle, that would be a one on one and I had to be the aggressor.

There it was the crew Detroit Industries had recruited for me. Somewhere behind that organization was the Chairwoman and just the fact they had recruited these three meant I had a path to the Chairwoman sitting there waiting for me. If I worked it right, I should be able to backtrack to that person and settle this matter once and for all.

Now I had a fairly good idea as to what was coming at me. What I had found out did not mean I was right, but I was willing to stake my life on my findings. Whatever, I was going to plan on this basis and also take into consideration there could well be others, and I needed to include in my planning.

Right now, only Tangle knew what he was getting himself into. I had decided I needed to take him out as soon as possible and I needed to do it with a mean spirit. Something that would make any others who may be involved stop and think twice and make them nervous and mistake prone. If I can do that, then they'll make mistakes and that is in my favor.

By this time, I had moved into full battle mode. I had my targets identified, well most of them anyway, and I was now ready to go after the Chairwoman and put together the means of identifying the individual. If nothing else worked out I was going to finish this one person off, even at my own death.

One thing I knew for certain was this thing was coming to a climax. All the real players had survived so far and now with each move, each action, there would be consequences. Like two fighters, circling one another, looking for the opening needed to make the knockout punch. No one was going to walk away from this thing whole. In order to win I would have to be willing to take a few shots myself. Yeah, this was one hell of a battle and a lot of people had died so far and it looked like a lot more were going to in the near future.

My own death, crap that was a forgone conclusion, I was good as dead and knew it. All I wanted were the Chairwoman and anyone else working under her. That is if Costello is not the Chairman. What a crap shoot, it was either or and I had better know before I committed myself.

It's funny, once you realize you're probably already dead, you seem to calm down and your mind clears. There's no interfering thought of how to survive and what to do in which scenario. That's all gone and survival is not the issue, the issue is getting even. The issue is taking them with you. The issue is leaving a path of death and destruction so wide even the blind could see it.

Well, that's what I'm paid for, to die that is. If I do then no one has to pay for the services rendered. If I survive then my pay will leave a rather large hole in their security budget for the next five or so years. I prefer to be paid and that is my sole plan at this time.

I have a contract even if they figure it was negated. I still had a contract and I was going to fulfill it to the letter even if I have to pin it to the Chairwoman's chest with a knife.

That was it, the battle lines are drawn and I know exactly what I have to do. This thing was not over, not by a long shot. Tangle may be my primary issue, but he no longer was the threat I felt he once was. I would deal with him as I do everything.

Slowly my mind set itself on the coming combat. Don't try to understand why we do what we do in this career, we just do it because it's our chosen career, and besides it pays good and frankly we, or I, love it.

What was about to happen had been seen before across the world where the finality of contractual obligation is brought to its final conclusion. In achieving that end there would be scarring in the region where the brunt of the action had taken place.

Here in the Detroit Industries Region the scarring had already started with the destruction of the Saturn building and the damage rendered to the Detroit Industries building. The fact is there was much more yet to come and there was no avoiding it.

Believe it or not I had five targets I was now working toward. You know who they are. There were the three contractors, Mr.

Costello and the Chairwoman, naturally there will be others, but those people will be the also ran's, the miscellaneous numbers that will be thrown in front of me to try and redirect me or possibly get in a lucky shot while in the process.

What was my best advantage? I was the predator and they were the prey, the ones on the defense. They were the ones looking behind their back while trying to set themselves up for me. They know who I am and they know what I can do and that is my best and most terrifying weapon.

I had no doubt they felt they were the predators, that's the way it works. You are always the predator and the other side is the prey. In this case, there was no doubt I was going to eat them alive. I was set and I was in the killing mode, it was time to kill and talk later.

Chapter Eight

Preparing for the Final Offensive

From this moment on nothing would take place during daylight hours. I had shifted to a night time offensive. Though it would help my opposition almost as much as it does me, it also placed me on the same level battlefield with them. The other side of the story was that Wicked was the best night time and darkness fighter in the world. It was my realm and I loved it.

During the daytime hours I remained in my hide away and worked on my research and planning. Each day I would work up my schedule for that night. In addition, I got my necessary eight hours sleep. I tried the set up a schedule that gave me a night plan for three nights in advance. That meant I needed to find and start tracking the other contractors and that turned out easier than I had anticipated.

I found Cheater first. This dumb kid was so sure of himself he just drove into town and got a room at the best hotel and then made himself at home. I still was not sure he had a contract, but his showing up almost ensured he did and I knew what it was for.

I would leave him alone for a while to ensure that Tangle wasn't using him as bait. Tangle was my biggest concern and he could have arrived here at any time and I wouldn't have known it. No, I was going to stay still and watch and wait.

Bouncer was a little more discrete in his arrival. He came in and stopped in the outskirts of the city and held up in a midlevel motel. Still, he was not that well versed in keeping himself off the radar. These new guys never seem to learn in this business the less visible, the better off you are. If they live long enough, they will eventually learn. Sure, as hell no one is going to tell them.

I set up my monitoring for the Detroit Industries and the three contractors. I expected little to nothing on Tangle, but I knew the other two would be on the hunt a good part of the time. Their methods were haphazard to say the least and not productive. No, I had little to worry about from them, but I had to understand they still could run across me, so I had to stay alert. Those two I could find in seconds so I concentrated on Tangle, and finding him.

On the other hand, Tangle didn't have to look for me. His game was to wait till I came to him and walked into his operation. Besides, he knew he could locate me when I dealt with the other two. All he had to do was follow them and they would bring him to me. That's his wicked little game, but he forgets when it comes to wickedness there is none like Wicked.

It was three days later when things started to get interesting. Cheater had been on the communicator all day trying to locate my base of operations. It was a futile effort on his part but was a great tracking system for me. He was moving all over the city at the time and I was sure Tangle was probably not too far behind him. Tangle was going to try and take me out while I dealt with Cheater or Bouncer. With that, I guess you could say I had two located and one roving free.

By this time, I had confirmed the number of contractors that were after me and it was the three, I had identified. It was time to start the show and I decided to take out Bouncer first. He had been working the old warehouse area for the past week trying to track my movements during the confrontation with Chad and Doper.

He had been able to find the detonation box on the dike, but that gave him nothing as far as I was concerned. The fact was, all he had to do was turn around and take a long hard look and he would find me.

I was taking my time with Bouncer knowing full well Tangle may not be with Cheater as he had been. He spent his time trying to anticipate my actions and moves. He had already figured I had gone night time on them and that was where he was putting his time. The same was true for Bouncer and so the odds of Tangle being nearby were good.

It was time, and Bouncer needed to go. I set my position and started my track on him. Tangle or no Tangle it was time to reduce the odds. As a hunter and being in the hunted position, such as I was, the hunter never really knows just what to expect. I knew what Bouncer was going to do and I could lead him to wherever I felt best to deal with him. At the same time, I was depending on Tangle to figure my game plan and be close by Bouncer. I had a special little gift for Tangle and when he got it, I would know exactly where he was. When that happens, the positions will be reversed and he will be the hunted.

Two days later Bouncer was working the back alleys one block west of the Saturn Futures collapsed building. I had no idea what he was thinking or why he was there unless he thought I was still working the Detroit Industries building. Whatever his reasoning, he was there and it was working into my move. Twenty minutes later I had him set and it was then I spotted the shadow. It was only a fleeting glimpse but it was there.

Tangle you wicked little man you know what's going on, what's about to happen now, don't you? Come on get in a little closer so I can leave a little gift for you. Bouncer was in a perfect position and I had him. His career was about to come to an end and my opposition was about to be reduced by one.

I held up and let Tangle move in closer. He could feel it. He knew I was there and Bouncer was about to fall. He was trying to position himself so he could see the whole event and in being able to do that spot me. To late Tang, you're mine and you're going to be left out of the game.

There I caught him again and he was in position. Good job, he had picked the one spot that had the best possible opportunity of spotting me when I moved. What he didn't know was I had anticipated his using that spot and my little gift for him was sitting there waiting. I counted down from five and then pushed the button.

This was not the death move on Tangle but it was a sign I had his number and he had no way around me. I wanted him to know what was coming and I wanted him to suffer some pain before it finally came to him, death that is.

It was just a small explosive but enough that would spread the fire gel over the whole of his hiding place. Not enough to kill him, but enough to hurt and make him pull away and leave Bouncer to me.

Bouncer first heard and then saw the charge go off and the man run out of the spot, on fire, and down the alley. He knew he was dead center in the line of fire but didn't know which direction it was going to come from.

By instinct he turned away from Tangle and headed right into my sights. I let him come ten more feet and then cut him down. Two rounds came in chest high hitting him body mass dead center and he was dead before he hit the ground.

That was it and I moved away and started back to my office. On the way I made a quick check on Tangle and I found him at his motel cleaning himself up. A check for Cheater and he was out at one of the high life bars enjoying himself. That was Cheater alright.

Tangle had now been notified the fight was on. He would not make that mistake again, but he also was on the psychological down side of our contest. He had been hit and he knew I had just tagged him. If I had wanted him dead, he would have been, right then and there.

The fact was I should have killed him then and there, but for some reason I wanted to play with him. I don't know if it was professional pride or just what, but I wanted him to suffer and feel the fear build up in his mind knowing full well I had him, I had set him up. He would know I could do it anytime and anyplace I wanted.

Now he was thinking, and if I knew Tangle, he was thinking he was not getting paid enough for this fight. It was now time to start tracking Tangle wherever he went. He was going to question the conditions of his contract and that meant more money. It also meant he would be contacting someone in the Detroit Industries organization to address the issue.

What about Cheater? Well, he would be fed into the mill when the time came and when it was best for Tangle. He tried to use Bouncer, but he made a mistake. The next time, when he used Cheater, he would not make a mistake. That is, if there were a next time.

Right now, everything was in a flux. So far, I had located and dealt with Bouncer and tagged Tangle. The truth was it accomplished little for me, other than putting Tangle on the defense. I need to know who they were working for and where they were.

It was around three that morning when I noted Tangle was on the move and it was out of town. I double checked on Cheater and found him in his room with a woman. I set out to follow Tangle and see what he was up to. We headed out of Detroit and toward

Dearborn about six to seven miles west of Detroit. Dearborn is where the power plant was said to be under development and manufactured. There was also a large management facility at the same location. Could it be we were going to find the Detroit Industries mind trust, the ones I needed to find?

He went directly to the Detroit Industries facility just north of down town Dearborn. He passed through the security gate and disappeared into the facility. There it was the place I needed to work on and the place I needed to gain entry into.

Right now, I could do nothing about Tangle and his meeting with those at the center, but I could start to scout the place and see just exactly what it was all about. It was huge. Besides manufacturing capabilities, it had a research and design facility as well. There had to be twenty thousand people working there. Bad news, because it meant it had a significant security system in it and the place was like a maze. Tangle would have it up on me there.

I had only one option and it was to settle back and take my time and observe. Tangle didn't know where I was or what I was doing. Until he got something that told him where I was at, he was not concerned.

This place was not the battleground I wanted, but the people I wanted were in there. Yet, that did not mean they were there all the time. Like most of the upper class they assumed contractors were too busy pursuing their contract to worry about where the uppers live or what they did. Right now, that's exactly what I wanted to know.

So, I sat and watched. I drove the perimeter of the plant and checked out all the access points. Finally, on the northeastern corner of the campus I found what I was looking for. It was the management entrance point. All right, that's enough for now of the Dearborn facility. I don't want to become fixated on the gate at this time. I will give it a few days and then return to carry out a close observation of those using the gate. Meanwhile I needed to take a better look at the region around the plant.

It was time to deal with Cheater and to set Tangle up. I would need him in order to get at the Chairwoman. I would have to give him his second lesson in how to kill someone without expending all my assets. He would be leading me to the Chairwoman and then dying

194

right there in front of his boss, the perfect ending to a friendship.

I knew who they were and who my prime target was. Tangle and Cheater were just a means of getting to my real targets. Now I was going to bring this thing to an end and in doing that I will demonstrate to those who had set this game in motion what it was like to live in real terror.

Right now, it didn't matter whether I survived or not, the point was they were going to die, to the last person, and Detroit Industries would cease to exist. The resulting void left with the collapse of Detroit Industries would spawn an industrial war the likes of which no one had ever seen. If I lived, I would be able to sit back and watch the carnage, if I did not live then I died knowing I had set the whole thing in motion.

I moved back into the Dearborn area starting at the management gate and moving out. I scouted every road and housing development within three miles of the gate. In moving through the area, I found the plant was sitting in a shallow valley that ran north and south, the management gate was on the east side. Just east of the gate and across the main north to south interchange, the terrain changed to rolling hills. Numerous roads ran up into these hills and serviced a number of homes and other buildings that faced the plant and the main gate.

It then came to me, which homes and buildings actually looked directly down on and into the management building which sat inside the plant and about a hundred yards from the gate. The management building was ten floors high and that put it on a level plane with many of the homes and buildings located on the hill directly across from it.

As I checked the area, I found three locations that fit the criteria I was working under, and so I concentrated on those three places. Each place would be perfect as an observation location for monitoring the plant. Two were residences and were valued at over a million and a half. Damn I'd love to have one like these. The office building was the third and it was perfectly located for an observation position. The sad part about it was one of those locations was destined to die, to be sacrificed in the midst of battle, but which one?

Listen, anyone who is planning an action like the one I was planning will always build in secondary coverage and support. The

196

houses and building on this hillside were perfectly positioned for providing direct and deadly cover for the management building on the plant site.

Wherever that location was it would be in a position to look directly at the top or Chairwoman's floor of the building or would be slightly elevated above that floor. The location would be in a position that would provide direct observation of anything going on within the top floor and in that way, one could monitor everything that went on in the management building. That location would also provide a platform for the stationing of snipers who could target anyone on the floor, especially in the Chairwoman's office.

That was it, I had the remainder of the tactics for the other contractors and security personnel of Detroit Industries set in my mind and it would work just fine for me as well. I must admit they did a fine job in selecting and targeting the top floor and the Chairwoman's office. Whatever they did to get me there it was going to be a trap and one impossible to escape from, so they thought.

It was their battle choice of terrain and not my choice so I would have to deal with that issue as well. It was now five days before the New Year break at the plant and I felt the assault at the plant would be best set for that time. I had this inner feeling that was their plan anyway.

Chapter Nine

Making the Move

I had followed Tangle to the Dearborn facilities and left him there as I returned to Detroit to deal with Cheater. I found Cheater at one of the more popular night spots in town and then set up waiting for him outside in the parking lot. No, I wasn't going to take him there. It was too open and too risky under the current situation.

As I set myself up it was approaching two in the morning and I knew the place would close up shortly after two. As they exited the club, I spotted Cheater with a woman and another couple. At first it appeared he had picked up a woman and they in turn picked up another couple.

As they approached their car, I noted all four were watching and looking. Yeah, they were a team and I would be taking the whole bunch out. I didn't like the woman thing, but I also knew more and more women were getting into the contract business, so if they wanted to play the game, they needed to face the same risks.

They exited the parking lot and headed east. After a block they pulled into an all-night restaurant, parked and got out and went in. I pulled on past the place and turned right at the next corner.

He hit me just as I was completing the turn, coming up directly behind me and ramming me. The blow knocked me sidewise and I got a look at Tangles eyes through his windshield. He poured it on and hit my driver's side door staying on top of me and pushing me down the street.

He then shoved his gun out the window and opened up on me. Damn he had me good and I had better start thinking soon or he was going to finish the game right then and there. I looked to my right and saw the next intersection coming up. As we approached the intersection I set up and timed my move and hit the gas just as we entered the intersection.

I was able to tear my rig away from him and head down the street as he continued to slide through the intersection. I needed five seconds and then I would make my escape good. He recovered quickly and was back on me in less time than I had anticipated. This was not good and I had better get this thing under control soon or he had me.

At the next intersection I set up to make a left turn. My plan was to take the turn and get my car around side ways to him as soon as possible and then open up on him. I started to concentrate on his windshield and driver's door window. That's where I needed to send my rounds.

I hit the intersection and got my setup perfect and made the turn I then swung around and shoved my .40 out the window and opened up on him. I fed the rounds to him as fast as I could pull the trigger. I was hitting him with everything I had right in the windshield and the driver's door. He had no alternative but to pull off.

He passed on through the intersection hitting my car with as many rounds as he could, but it gave me my out and I took advantage of it. I broke off and headed in the opposite direction from Tangle. I knew if I could make two turns on him, I had him and that's exactly what happened. I then killed my lights and continued out of town and south. I drove another 50 miles before turning east and heading for my safe house.

Once I had the car garaged, I went into the house and sat down. What the hell just happened out there anyway? Tangle had me like he knew just exactly where I was at. He came off the side street full throttle almost as if he knew I would be there when he got there. It was not one of those, out of the blue I didn't know you were there, things. He knew I was there.

That meant one of two things, he had Cheater marked or he had me marked. Shit, he could be here right now and he would have me. I grabbed my scanner and went to the garage and scanned the car, it was clean. No, he had Cheater marked and figured I would be working him next. Still the manner in which he took me told me it was something more. What the hell was it?

I needed to sit down and think this thing out. There was something going on here that had changed the balance of the game and Tangle had the advantage now. What was it? What had I done in the past few hours or the past day that would change things as it has? I needed to review my movements over the last 24 hours in detail and do it now. There was no way I could return to Detroit and deal with these people until I had this worked out.

It took me five hours before it finally hit me. It was not my going to Dearborn, it was related to Cheater and the only thing that it could be was that Tangle was monitoring Cheater. How was he doing that? How could he monitor Cheater and then shift over to me?

Damn it was a puzzle and I needed to consider everything concerning the area where I had been monitoring Cheater. If he wasn't tagged and I wasn't tagged then what was it? What was there about this area of town that made it possible to locate and track someone or a group of people?

My mind went to Detroit and I started looking at the streets and the traffic movement. As I thought about it, I got to thinking about the movement of traffic through the area and then it started to register on me. He could see us. He could actually see our vehicles moving through the city streets and that meant only one thing, video.

Yeah, that was it, he was using the security camera system for the city to track

Cheater and while doing that he spotted me. That had to be it, but how the hell was he doing that. How the hell could he? It then hit me. Hell, yes, he was and it was being done by Detroit Industries.

All right, they were now working in coordination with one another. Cheater was the bait and Detroit Industries was watching Cheater and looking for me. That changed everything. I needed to figure a way to deal with this issue and try and turn it to my advantage. It was time for Wicked to get wicked.

Back to the computer, and I started working up the City of Detroit. As I moved through their web site, I found the traffic control section and then moved into the video monitoring system. There was a map layout of the city that marked the location of every street mounted video camera. In addition, it marked the location of every parking lot camera and public building entrances camera.

It was a maze of cameras that covered the entire city, yet it did not cover everything. There were blank areas, areas with no camera coverage and there were a lot of them. This was not a system setup to track everything that happens all over the city it was a general monitoring system. That meant I should be able to skirt the cameras and move around the city without any problem.

I would become invisible again and free to go about my task of clearing up this mess. Now it was Tangle's turn to wonder what the hell happened.

After studying the camera layout of the city, I found a pattern in the layout of the cameras. They were set up on a grid system with all the even number streets being covered intersection by intersection. That left the odd numbered streets clear and gave me access to what I wanted.

It wasn't long before Tangle had determined I was running in the shadows again. We were back to a level battleground now. So, it was back to business and the game was back on. This time it was going to be different. This time Tangle had to go.

Again, it was like two fighters circling one another trying to find an opening either one could take advantage of. Both knew the wrong choice would probably result in their being knocked out. So, who was going to blink first? The truth was I loved this kind of game. It required me to produce the best of my skills and match them against my opponent. It sharpened my mind and brought the degree of concentration I needed out and to the forefront.

It would come three days later and believe it or not it would be Cheater who would tip the balance between Tangle and I. I had moved the emphasis of my action out into the Dearborn area and this particular night I was working the executive gate watching for any sign of the Chairwoman.

My particular location was deep into a wooded area north of the gate and overlooking the parking lot across the street from the gate. I saw the dark rig moving across the parking lot across from the gate first. It was crawling along as if it were stalking something. It was then I saw the car on the street. It was the same car Cheater had been driving the night Tangle and I tangled.

If that was Cheater then the other car was Tangle and I knew I was set. I had a clear field of fire on both vehicles and had decided to target Tangle when both rigs came together at the gate. Cheater turned into the gate and Tangle crossed the road out of the parking lot to the gate. They both went in and continued on across the tarmac to the main office pavilion. They disappeared behind the building. I had decided to hold my fire I needed to be closer to them.

There was only one reason for them to be there and that was at the summons of the Chairwoman. They were all there in that building at the Dearborn plant. Everything was there waiting for me. It was the perfect setup and the perfect time. December 31, 2173. The plant was shut down and empty for the New Year's Holiday.

They wouldn't be leaving the plant any time soon; I was sure of that. No this was the way it was supposed to be and it was all set up for me. A trap, yeah, a trap and I was going to walk right into it. Why? Because I knew it was the right thing to do and everything was primed for the taking, whether they thought so or not.

I left my position and moved back up and over the ridge and to my car. I drove down off the ridge area and on to the access road and approached the gate. There was one guard in the gate house as I approached. The gate was down and as I drove up to it, he stepped out of the guard house and signaled me to stop. He took two steps toward me before the .40 rounds hit him and put him down. I got out of the car and pushed the gate button and got back in the car and started across the tarmac for the main office building.

As I approached the building, I could see lights on in the office windows on the top floor ten stories up. The rest of the building was dark. I wouldn't be going to the tenth floor. They were waiting for me on the first. That would be where the fight would take place and some or all of us would die.

I drove straight to the building and parked at the center of it and left my car. I walked up to the nearest window and kicked it in and entered the building. Once inside the game was on and there would be no truces called.

The area I entered into was an open office area filled with desks and area partitions. I would say the area in total covered at least half the foot print of the building. I stayed low and waited listening for anything that would give me a clue as to where Cheater and Tangle were.

Tangle wouldn't come right at me but Cheater would. No Tangle would wait until all the indicators were there to ensure him, he had the game won. There was nothing, it was dead silent. Well not really, there were other sounds.

I could hear the air coming from the heating system. Over to my right was a clock ticking on a desk and further beyond that was a desk fountain. You know one of those little things that bubble and makes those soft water noises that seems to calm people.

Off to the left was a vending machine and refrigerator. There were numerous other odd sounds and noises in the area but nothing I could tie to a human. The first floor appeared to be empty and that meant I would be working my way up to the top floor.

It changed everything. I had nine floors over me and Cheater or Tangle could be on any one of the nine. I would either find both of them on the same floor or each one would take a floor and set up for me. I was sure they would be working a floor each on their own.

The problem I was having was the fact the place was so quiet. This place was crawling with security and the other two contractors. The fact was they wanted me to work my way into their trap, and once they had me, I was beginning to think they planned on using me for something else and not just to kill me off.

From my perspective, and I was accustomed to that. I was going to die in that building tonight or they had other plans for me I would rather not consider. So, the only way to work in this situation was to set the place up for a total take down. By that I meant I was going to take each floor one at a time. The one thing that was not going to happen was taking me alive.

I moved back out the window I came in and returned to my car and opened the trunk. I took two large backpacks out of the trunk and returned to the interior of the building. I was now ready to head up to the other floors and work my way into their trap.

I located the elevators and stairways for the building and then started to work. I entered each elevator and placed charges in the control panel set to go off when the down button was pushed. It took several minutes to load both elevators. I had to remove the control panel and then place the charges down inside the panel and then place my wire clips on the down button. Why the down button? Well, the elevators were on the first floor and if anyone needed them, they had to bring the selected elevator up to the floor they were on. It would be when they started down when the charge would go off. I had brought each unit to the first floor and left them there.

I then went to each of the three stairwells and started my set up. I decided to access each floor from the end stairwell and work up the building, checking each floor out and welding each stairwell door shut. I made sure I switched ends each time I started up to the next floor.

This way by using thermite charges I could weld each door shut as I came on to the floor. Then I would stop at the central stairwell and weld that door shut. I continued to check each floor out and then when I started up to the next floor, I would weld the last door shut.

Each floor would require an end-to-end search to make sure I was not leaving someone behind me. If that happened then I was in serious trouble. It was a process that would take time and I'm sure would start to make those above me a little more nervous as each minute passed. That was all right, because when someone is nervous, they're prone to make mistakes and in this game a mistake is a killer.

It was on the third floor when I found and dealt with my first security unit. As I stepped out of the stairwell, I could smell them. They were scared spit-less but I admired the fact they stayed with it. It would do them little or no good, but I still admired them. What they didn't know and I knew was they were being fed to me in hopes a lucky shot would take me out. That wasn't going to happen.

It was a three-man team and they were poorly trained. They stuck together and failed to cover their entire perimeter. It was a turkey shoot. All three died quietly and quickly. Their presence only confirmed what I was sure of. This was clearly a trap and now I was beginning to think the Chairwoman was not anywhere in or around this building.

Each floor now had security units on them and they varied in size and number. When were these people going to learn feeding these units to a contractor only enhanced his ability to continue on? It told me more about my opposition than it helped them. As I cleared each floor that left those above with only one way to go and that was up. In effect I was sweeping everyone in front of me up and toward the top floor.

I could feel him when I came onto the seventh floor. Yeah, Cheater was there, but not Tangle. He was waiting for me on top, on the tenth floor, maybe. But right now, I was going to deal with Cheater. He was here alone. There were no other security people on the floor. It was then I heard one of the elevators start up the building. I stayed put and listened and waited as the unit made its way up.

It passed the seventh and continued passed the eight and then stopped at the ninth. It stayed there. I waited another five minutes but it remained on the ninth floor. If they had been planning on going down to the first or coming down to me, they changed their minds. Eventually someone would use the elevator, and when they did. I put that in the back of my mind and then moved on. Cheater was waiting for me.

In time, a well experienced contractor develops many ways of dealing with an opponent. One of the best is his ability to feel his opponent. Every sense in his body is conditioned to reach out and feel, smell, hear, see, and taste the environment he is working his way through. You learn to recognize the thoughts and feelings of your opponent. You can feel when they start to build for the coming encounter. Their heart rate increases as does their respiratory process.

Yeah, Cheater was there and he was ready. He was keyed up and watching for that small indication as to just where I was at. He was looking for Wicked and wicked he was about to find.

I was halfway down the hall and approaching the elevators when I sensed his movement. He was in the stairwell just before the elevators. That door is to my left and just before the first elevator. I could see the stairwell door was open just a crack so that he could ease the door open and see me moving down the hallway toward him.

No, he wasn't going to crack open the door he was going to jerk it open at the right time and in the process cause me to over react and give him that second, he needed to put me down. He needed to move fast in hopes it would surprise me and distract me from my situation. In that fraction of a second he would take me.

I moved across the hall to my left side and put my back against the wall and slid down the hallway approaching the door to the stairwell, keeping the door knob in my sight, still paying attention to the areas around me and down the hallway. I needed to move slowly and give myself all the leeway possible so I could see any movement as it happened.

It started with a small almost unperceivable movement of the door knob. He was there and he was prepping for the pull. I stopped and crouched down and leveled my .40 on the door right where the knob was and where the door separated from the jam as he pulled it open. His gun would come through first and would be firing I would open up after his second round.

When it started everything slowed to a snail's pace. I waited as round one went off and followed a second later by round two and then Cheaters body. He was good, but I had him anticipated and he was dead meat as well. I opened up on his body as he was coming from behind the door and its momentum was pushing him forward and through the door.

As my rounds found the mark, he tried to adjust his direction of fire. He knew he had blown it and was shooting way over my head and body but it was too late. My third round hit him in the neck and blew out his spine as it exited. Everything turned off at that time and he started down.

It really is hard to watch a career come to an end like this. He wasn't a bad guy, just a guy trying to do his job and make a living. The only problem was he took the wrong contract and that put him and me on the wrong side of the game. Too bad, I could have taught him a lot over the years. Anyway, number one is down.

I moved over and checked the body and then pulled him into the hallway and set the thermite charge in the door and moved on. I got to the end of the hallway when I heard the elevator door open and then close. I moved into the stairwell and braced myself against the wall and away from the door.

Sure, as hell, whoever it was hit the down button and all hell busted loose. Whoever it was got his ride down but it was at full speed with no stops on the way down. I heard the unit drop and several seconds later it hit the bottom of the shaft.

That took place on the ninth floor so the damage here on the seventh was minor just the elevator door being bulged out a bit.

I moved to the eighth floor and stood there at the door several seconds listening and feeling for someone, anyone. It was quiet and so I set the next thermite charge and entered the hallway. The damage to this floor was considerable. The elevator door was blown off the frame and lying on the floor. There was considerable dust and smoke floating throughout the floor.

Anyone who had been on this floor was feeling the effect of the blast. I'm sure their ears were ringing and they were having a little trouble breathing clean air. This was good because it would mask my presence on that floor and make my job much easier.

I felt no one on this floor. That didn't mean there was no one here, the results of the explosion could well cover their presence.

Realizing that, I knew Tangle was there waiting for me. He knew full well I would charge the elevators and he also knew the ninth and eighth floors would be filled with covering smoke and dust when the bomb went off. That made those two floors perfect for this confrontation. This was the ultimate involvement and only one would come out alive.

My first job was to get onto the floor without his taking me out. I knew he was watching the stairwells and also knew he couldn't cover all three at once. It was a crap shoot as to which stairway he was watching and which one I came out of. It's one of those rolls of the dice things and I rolled.

So far everything was with me. I moved across the hall to the first door and entered the room. As I looked around, I found this floor, at least this side of the floor, was the open space concept as well. With the haze of the explosion in the air and minimal light from a few nights light along the walls it was difficult to see. I would need all my senses in this situation and they needed to be right on.

The first round came in from the far end of the floor. It was more of a search round trying to get me to fire back and give my position away. When he fired the shot, he was diagonal to me and at the other end of the floor from me. By now he could be over to my left or across the hall. There was no indication of the door opening and so I felt sure he was still in this office area.

I moved over to the center of the room and started moving toward the other end of the floor. It was around a hundred fifty feet to the other end of the building with this open area being around a hundred feet wide. There were easily twenty to twenty-five work stations in this area and each one was cover for a person or persons.

I sat down behind a desk and stilled myself and started to listen. Once I identified the background noise I then started to concentrate on any other sounds as they came about. Tangle was good at stealth and he could be on top of you before you knew it. The only difference was I had an acute sense of hearing and I could feel people as they moved around me. Every sense was elevated and on total alert.

Then I found him. He was not close but he was there working his way toward me. But it wasn't Tangle. No there was another there and he was working in tandem with Tangle. I set his sound aside and concentrated on Tangle. Yeah, he was there moving down the window side of the room and just back from the other. He was setting up for me while I was dealing with the other and he would then come in on me at that time.

I moved around the desk I was behind and made the move to the side Tangle was on. That spaced me away from the other and into Tangles side of the room. I needed to be in as close a proximity to Tangle as I could get. That put him in jeopardy as well from the other and he had two fire sources to worry about.

I settled in again and listened, I could hear the breathing of the other and he was almost directly across from me on the hallway side of the open work area. That would put Tangle to my left and no more than twenty feet away from me and toward the windows.

I sat there and looked up at the windows and then saw a slight movement in the glass of the window. It was his back and he was just two desks over from me. The other had moved on and was approaching the wall by this time. His breathing was now labored as he became aware, he had no idea where I was at.

I calmed myself and set my weapon for Tangle and waited. There he was coming around the end of the line of desks and moving right into my sights. The other had grounded and didn't know which way to go. Tangle knew the other had found nothing and so he figured I was close by, but just how close, he wasn't sure.

It was now, and the time was here for this confrontation to come to an end. He moved around the end of the desk and I swung around in the same direction and dropped to the floor in front of him and opened up. He opened up just a heartbeat behind me. I saw my rounds hit and on the third one I put that round through his forehead. He got two rounds off and one found its mark in my left side.

I swung around as the other came up over the desks and I cut loose on him. He had four rounds in him before he cleared the top of the desk. He wasn't able to get a round off and was dead before he hit the floor. I swung back around and put two more rounds into Tangle. Everything fell quiet. I moved over to the corner by the window and checked out my wound. He hit me in the left side just above the hip. That was the intestinal region and I didn't know if he had damaged my intestines or not. I felt around and found the bullet just under the skin in my back. I didn't think he had done any more damage than just the hole in the fleshy part of the lower abdomen.

I pulled a wound pack out, stuck it in place and wrapped the bandage in place and pulled my shirt back down and around the bandage. I sat there waiting to see if anyone else moved into the area. After maybe five minutes I determined there were no others there so I started to move toward the far end of the floor and the stairwell to the ninth floor.

I made it to the far stairwell and set the thermite charge and moved up toward the ninth floor. I had no idea what would be waiting for me but I knew I was getting closer to the answers to the many questions I had.

As I prepared to enter the ninth floor the thermite charge on the last door of the eighth floor went off. I pushed the door to the ninth floor open and slid in on the floor. The central area of the floor had severe damage due to the elevator charge going off here. I saw a hand on the floor next to the elevator. As I moved over several feet, I saw the rest of the body under the elevator door.

I calmed myself and listened. It was quiet as a tomb. Nothing was moving on this floor and that bothered me even more. The entire floor was open space except for the central region which was made up of the square that housed the central stairwell and the elevators and restrooms for that floor. The rest of the space was taken up by desks.

I decided to move around the perimeter of the floor to check everything out. It was clear and I then moved to the central core and placed thermite charges in the stairwell door and moved off toward the opposite end of the floor and the stairwell to the top or tenth floor.

I came out on the tenth floor in a hallway. At the far end of the floor, just past the elevators, was a double door that sat across the hallway. The rest of the floor was closed off with offices. I would be checking each and every office as I moved down the hallway.

I thermite charged the stairwell door and moved to the next office door. I slid into the office and found it empty. I came back out and thermite charged the door and moved on. Welding each door closed as I moved toward the double doors ahead of me.

I finally reached the double doors and checked the stairwell at that location and then readied myself for entry into the Chairwoman's office.

Right then I needed to stop. It was a good location in that I had all entrances to that area closed off and I had the entrance to the Chairwoman's office area covered. I needed to check my wound again and make sure I had it covered and it was not bleeding. I didn't want it to become a problem once I was facing the staff and boss inside of those office doors.

This was it; everything had been set up and I had complete control of the whole of the building, except for the area behind the door. I let my mind clear and I prepared to make entry. I would be approaching that door and fully expected to find a security unit on the other side.

I checked my clip and pulled it and put in a fresh one. I made sure the backpack was secured and the single duffle bag I had left was right there at my feet. It was time and this was the end of a long hard contract. No matter what happened from this point on there would be no one other than me, if I survived, leaving these offices.

The trap had not been completely sprung yet. I knew the real bait was there inside the office door and once I was inside that office area and in control of it then and only then would the final chapter in this contest take place. They had it planned but they did not have me planned.

Damn I love endings like this. Everyone's had their shot and we're now to the final minutes and the final movements on the game board. We both had a check going but only one would get the check mate.

My mind was running over all that had happened since I had entered the building. I was trying to review and make sure I had left nothing out. The fact of the matter was I was on the top floor of a building in the Dearborn plant of the Detroit Industries manufacturing facility.

That was like being the lone green pea on a pile of yellow corn. Yeah, I was all alone and if I survived, I still had to go down ten floors, get to my car, head for the gate and exit the area without being seen or contacted by the company security system.

So, no matter what happened here on the tenth floor I was probably not going to get out of this thing without running into half the company's army of security personnel. That was a most comforting thought in itself. Well, that's something I'll worry about at that time, right now I needed to deal with the issue at hand and finish this thing once and for all.

I just needed to rest a few more minutes before taking on this final issue. I was tired and wounded and not really too interested in continuing on. It would have been so easy to just lay it down right there and let things end. That is if I wasn't Denton Wicked.

Reputation, that was one of my major issues. I had a reputation and I had to keep it up. Professional position required I maintain it and that can be a problem. Really, it can be. Here I am standing at the final door to the end of this thing and I'm talking about reputation.

The fact is, I have no other way to go. I have to go through that door and deal with whatever is on the other side. What they don't know is I still have a few surprises for them once I get in there. We will see how this goes.

Chapter Ten

Hunting the Chairwoman to Ground

So far, the fight had been intense and painful. Cheater and Tangle had fallen along with a number of other security personnel. Now I found myself on the tenth floor and outside the offices of the Chairwoman of the Board of Detroit Industries. All that was running through my mind was the last time I contacted the Chairwoman, and found later on I had the wrong person.

I didn't even know if the person was on the premises or whether that person was actually male or female. I guess my first problem was to make entry and then sort things out from there. I tried the door and it was unlocked and so I pushed it open and stepped back and away from the door expecting any number of rounds to come through the door as I opened it. There was nothing it was dead quiet. I slowly looked into the area on the other side of the door finding a waiting area that was empty. Even the reception desk was empty.

I pushed on into this area and then moved across to the inner doors. As I moved across the lobby, I scanned for video cameras and there they were, except they were pointed down at the floor below them.

At the inner door I tried the handle and it too was unlocked. What the hell anyway. Up till now the security and resistance had been extensive but now there was nothing. I looked inside and there across the room was the largest glass desk I had ever seen. A quick check of the rest of the area resulted in no one being present.

Behind the desk were the windows of the tenth floor looking out over the factory buildings of the Dearborn facilities. To the right were a second set of windows looking out over the parking lot or tarmac and facing the hills across the road from the plant.

Standing at those windows with her back to me was one lone subject. I moved into the room and across to the desk stopping there watching her. "Welcome Mr. Wicked, I see you've finally found your way to my office."

For a moment I couldn't talk. "Yes, it was somewhat difficult but I managed to make it. Am I on time?"

She didn't move, just kept looking out the window. "Yes, you're right on time would you like to take a seat?"

"No right now I prefer to remain standing. May I ask a question?"

"By all means, ask your question."

She still hadn't move but did turn her head about a quarter turn to the right as she answered my question.

"What the hell was this whole thing all about?"

She quietly turned halfway to me and looked at me. "I don't believe we have that much time for a detailed answer Mr. Wicked. But I can tell you it was all planned and you have fulfilled your part of that plan completely."

There we were standing at the top of a totally destroyed building also loaded with additional explosives and she is still talking as if the game was still in full force. One thing I knew right then and there I was in a position that had no way out, I was standing in a box, with little or no means of gaining my escape. I had made up my mind she was going to go with me no matter what happens.

It was then she turned slowing toward me. I looked at her and thought back those four months and recalled going to the Detroit Industries building to sign the contract papers. She was the receptionist on the first management floor as I left the elevator. "You're the receptionist?"

She smiled at me and nodded her head. "I find it better to move around the building from time to time and fill other positions to see just how things are going. It also makes for an easy exit if and when I find the need."

"You know I could kill you before anyone could get to me to stop me, don't you?"

She continued to smile and nod her head. "Yes, I guess you could but you won't. Mr. Wicked you're not in a position to take any action against me. You have been used to achieve a specific goal and anything beyond that will result in nothing of any significance. In fact, you have the opportunity of walking out of this place and to live a happy and a retired lifestyle if you so desire."

She had started to move from the window and over to the left to the chair across from me and in front of the east windows and then sat down. Right then three red dots appeared on my chest. I looked at her and smiled. "So, I'm in a trap and if I play this right I'll leave here with your blessings?"

She looked up at me. "No, if you do it right you will leave here alive. I will never see you again and this world will be safer without you. There's no blessing in this Mr. Wicked. It's just you leaving and getting out of my way."

"Then what the hell did you achieve other than getting a building destroyed and a large number of people killed?"

"Time Mr. Wicked time, we needed more time to complete our repositioning of our control over the new technology we have discovered. That required time and you gave that to us. Nothing can stop Detroit Industries from gaining a major control position in the world now."

That was it, not a new weapon system or a new power system. Those were the bait, but the real target was the acquisition of a greater power base and that's worth twenty weapons systems in itself.

This little bitch was savvier than I had thought and she played us contractors well, the only problem I saw was she was far too sure of herself and that was her weakness.

I leaned across the table toward her. "You're Ms. Worthington, is that right?"

She smiled at me and sat back. "Yes Mr. Wicked my name is Worthington, Bradley R."

She had a level of pride in her voice as she said that. I continued. "Well, I have to congratulate you for your skill in playing this game out. However, you have missed one little issue here and if you would allow me, I will tell you what that is?"

The smile left her face as she watched me. The red spots were still on my chest and following me inch by inch as I moved in place. "Yes Mr. Wicked I can give you that amount of time before we end this game."

"Thank you. To start with I was rather unhappy with the way you started this thing out. You picked me specifically for this setup and frankly it makes me madder than hell but, leaving that behind us, I have to inform you, you have not really done your homework because you have failed to understand the professional standards of a contractor.

"We are a proud profession. In addition, we are a brutal profession and understand we could die at any moment of any day. We are all well acquainted with one another and many of us have worked together over the years. Maybe you didn't know it but Cheater and Bouncer and I were good friends. They were rather young, but I liked them both. Tangle and I had been close and had grown apart these last ten years. In fact, Tangle was my brother, yes, my real brother.

"We are all close and lived in a brotherhood few have access to. We know our work will bring us across one another's trails, and those crossings could result in one or both of us dying. That you have seen a lot of the past few days. I guess I'm trying to tell you death is a part of our lives, as much as living is. So, you see it's no problem setting things up even if it meant our own death."

At that moment I stood back up and reached up and started to open my coat. The red dots were repositioning themselves on my chest. As I pulled the coat open, she started to push back away from the desk. There before her I had on a vest which was loaded up with thirty-five pounds of military grade high explosives. "You see whether I kill you with my bare hands or they shoot me first, this thing goes off. Oh, a head shot won't work people. When I entered this office, I tripped a switch and the vest will go off if my heart or brain stops. No matter what happens here at this time, young lady, you and I are going to die here together."

Her face was ashen as she sat there looking at the vest of explosives. "You can't mean that? You're insane, do you know that?"

"Young lady, it makes little or no difference whether I'm insane or not. I knew the moment I came through that gate out there I would never leave this place alive. My sole desire was to end up here in your presence with the final act of paying you back for all you have done these past months.

"You have seen to the death of a lot of people during this time. No, you're far more corrupt than any contractor could ever be. You see I really don't care what Detroit Industries accomplishes one way or the other. The end result will be more working classes being subjected to your brutal domination.

"No this is a personal thing to me and one I have worked long and hard for. You've given me the opportunity to do something about the brutal actions of some of the industry across this world. What is going to happen here tonight will result in a worldwide war that will drive industry to the brink of total ruin. I would even go as far as to say a new era is about to come up on the earth and industry will play a minor role in it.

"That young lady, will be your legacy to mankind. You were far too smart and over confident and that made you the perfect tool for a reconfiguration of this world. Whether I played into your hands or you into mine makes little difference to you and me at this time. What is important is you and I cast the first rock in the battle that is going to be ignited across the world this day. For that I thank you."

She sat there looking at me and then turned and looked out the window. She stood up and walked to the window and stopped. "I guess you've finally had your revenge. So maybe I had better let you in on a little secret right now."

She turned back toward me. "My name is Worthington, but I'm not the Chairman. No, I'm what everyone was supposed to think was the Chairwoman. Actually, he sits out there across the tarmac in that office building facing us. If you look closely you will see the laser lights coming from the top floor of the building."

I moved around the desk and to the window and looked out across the tarmac. "Right, Mr. Costello's building."

I felt her jerk as she looked up at me. "What did you say?"

I looked down at her. "I said that's Mr. Costello's office building. You know that little short fat guy who works down in finance. That slime ball who crawls around in the entrails of this company hiding like the little creep he is?

She looked back toward the building and just then I saluted and pressed the button in my left hand. There was a flash and then a bright white light lit up the sky and surrounding woodlands as the building came apart at the seams.

The laser lights went out and the building collapsed in on itself as fire engulfed it. I turned and walked over to the other side of the desk and turned back facing her. She had turned and walked to the back of the chair and just stood there.

The look on her face was total confusion as she tried to grasp what had just happened. I guess when all your plans go up in flames it is rather hard to take it all in. "Ms. Worthington the war of the world has started. I would suggest you find a place to hold up and get out of the way, especially here at Detroit. This place will be the first to see the reality of war."

"You're not going to kill me?"

I turned to walk out the door and then looked back at her. "No, I don't think that will be necessary at this time. We've all been used in this game and it's time for each of us to re-evaluate where we're at and what our future is.

"For me I have reached a point where I just want to sit down and write about this life and what the new world had left behind. The contractor is a lost and dead breed now and I hope I can instill in those who follow to never let that system show its ugly head again.

"Good evening young lady and I wish you all the luck in the days ahead, you'll need them."

I left her standing there wondering just what the hell happened. Poor kid she had little life experience and now she has lost it all. I had found my Chairman and taken the appropriate action against him. I checked my accounts and found the proper deposit had taken place; the contract was fulfilled. I had successfully laid waste to the Detroit Industries and taken their predatory Chairman out, job complete.

As I approached the two remaining elevators, I disconnected the explosive packets in both of them and then took one down to the first floor and then went out to my car and started across the tarmac. There were no additional security people. Other than the burning remains of a small office building across the road from the management gate, all was quiet.

I returned to my hideaway and cleaned up. It had been a hard battle and I had been wounded. After tending the wound and then taking a nice long hot shower I sat down at my desk and went over the overall actions of the last four months.

Today was the first day of a new year and I had at least three months before the next contract could be expected. Yes, I'm a wicked person. Telling that poor kid all those stories about the coming war and my upcoming death. It seemed to make it easier for her to let go and clear out of the area and start a new life.

The Detroit Industries situation had finally quieted down and stabilized. New management moved in and everything was back to status-quo. I had made a good profit from the contract and on top of that got rid of a couple of my competitors. Most of all I got Tangle out of my life and that of every other contractor out there. There was little grief over his passing.

Yes, there was a major weapons development by the Saturn Futures industry and Detroit had tried to steal it. We had destroyed that developmental system but managed to save the power generating system.

Everyone will benefit from this program. If Detroit Industries had not been so greedy in regards to those two projects there never would have been a contract let on the Chairman and his supporters including the contractors who had signed with him.

The only one to walk away from the Detroit group was Ms. Worthington and I learned four days later she had been contacted and placed under arrest. The agreement had been to not kill her, but that did not remove the fact she needed to pay and so a term in prison was ordered for her.

Maybe I should have taken care of her myself. Time in prison sometimes is not that pleasant. I'm a hardnosed contractor but in her case, I found my soft side. She had fallen in with Costello and he had sold her on what Detroit Industries was doing.

At her age these kids can be easily manipulated into a false sense of loyalty both between them and their boss. Costello had done just that and then took advantage of her. She committed herself to him and almost died as a result.

No, it's best she learns her lesson in this case and a time in prison will do just that. She'll have a chance to regain her reputation and career after her prison time but for now she must pay the price for her belief in the wrong man.

It always feels good when you've achieved a successful contract. This one was particularly generous in the amount that was placed into my account. I received five times what I normally charged and that in itself made me a rather wealthy man.

In addition, they paid me for my costs and losses. That came to another half a million when I consider the two houses and warehouse that had been destroyed. I was in a position where I could leave this area and find a good place to settle down and take some time off.

There would be a new generation of contractors coming on line now and I would still contract, but I had the top choice of what I wanted and how much I was to receive for my services. Life was looking really good.

Chapter Eleven

We Were All Conned

The name of the game is secrets, your ability to keep them and break them. In this case we had to keep the real secrets behind this Detroit Industries issue. In the end we were more than just a little successful. We stopped the move by Mr. Costello and broke the back of Detroit Industries. That left a huge void the other local industries set to work filling. None wanted to take over, they preferred to move everything back to status-quo.

When Detroit Industries hired me, they figured I was not anything in particular. They knew of my reputation but they did not relate that to my knowledge or intelligence. They figured me to be a sluggard and brute. Yeah, I'll kill without remorse or feelings, but that does not make me a brute. They thought wicked of Wicked and paid the price.

The lesson to be learned here was whenever Wicked is working an area, do not underestimate him. You try anything wicked with me and I'll teach you what Wicked is all about. I am what I am and those who underestimate me pay the highest price. Cheater, Bouncer, Doper, Chad and Tangle, all jumped on the side with the most money and never considered the motives behind it. They went for the money, well maybe Tangle didn't. He has always wanted me and this was his greatest chance to take me out. Bad move on his part.

Well, I guess it's time to let the rest of the story out. There is one more detail left in the contract. Now everything is back to normal or as near normal as it can be, I now have to locate the individual who was responsible for the weapons systems at Saturn Futures. That person walked off early with a lot of money. It was the money he demanded that created the necessity for Detroit Industries to try a takeover. He started this thing and now he's going to pay.

I had his name, Jacobi Stillman, and the last place he lived was in the Dearborn area. My job was to pursue and bring him to ground, literally. Everything I have found out about this guy has confirmed he used his weapons design to draw Detroit Industries into a deal with him. He collected a large sum of money then gave over the controlling codes and access code to Saturn Futures, called Powerhouse, and then skipped out.

This creep needs to be found and then dealt with. My problem is he is said to have a well-trained security unit covering him. When I worked my sources, I believe his primary contractor is one Iddings Quinton also known as Teacher. I've never met Teacher but I've heard a lot about him and if even half is true then I'll have my hands full.

The problem is he doesn't know me either and so we will be meeting on level grounds. I still want to pick the battlefield. No matter, Jacobi must pay and that's my contract for now. I was fairly certain he had not moved that far. While checking my sources I had learned Teacher had left his home country of New Zealand and probably was here in the North American area. It would take little to check the airport for his arrival time and location.

I first needed more background on Jacobi. As I researched him, I found he had three PhDs and all were in the scientific fields. No wonder he was a top flight weapons designer. The next thing I found was he was young. As it turned out he is a child prodigy and he attained his first PhD in physics when he was seventeen years old. I had a brain working against me and that meant I would need to be up on my chess game for sure.

Currently he is twenty-seven years old and single. Further checks on his family showed none. It appeared he had no siblings and his parents were missing as well. That caused me to go back into his school records and find everything I could on his family there.

Sure, enough I found his parents, and he did have a sister by the name of Bradley. That stopped me short, was that the same Bradley, no it couldn't be. Yet, it would fit perfect with this mess. Damn, then it hit me that was the tie between Costello and him, it was Bradley. Hell, she was into this thing deeper than I had imagined.

I made a check as to which prison she was in and learned they had been able to negotiate a delayed prison sentence for her to give her time to take care of a number of personal needs. Yeah, they were personal needs alright. I'll bet my entire contract she was with her brother at this time and where they were was a mystery.

I had no idea as to whether the two of them were actually dangerous or whether they were just trying to avoid the world and live their own lives. I still had the contract and I still needed to find Jacobi and deal with him, but what about Bradley. All right I'll wait until I find them before I deal with that decision. That gives me all the leeway I needed to deal with her when the time comes.

Next on my list of concerns is the fact Jacobi managed to slip out on us. He probably managed to take the plans and developmental research for the weapon and power unit with him as well. If so, then he has the ability to produce that weapon and use it, maybe not as readily as Detroit Industries could have, but good enough to be a problem.

Ok, things were really beginning to look bad. I had a rogue scientist with all the money he would ever want, the plans and ability to produce a weapon the likes of which this world had never seen and he had his sister with him and she was capable of just about anything.

And, for his protection he has brought on board one Iddings Quinton, better known as Teacher as his protection. Maybe we need to talk about Teacher for a few.

His name describes him to a tee. Teacher and he could teach just about all of us a thing or two. As I researched him, I discovered a man who had been in this business for a long time, probably longer than anyone I knew. As I said before, longevity in this business creates skill and knowledge and that he had. As I researched Teacher it became clear this person was the nightmare of all contractors.

Jacobi had taken his time and set this thing up well. From all I could find out about Teacher he was tenacious and never ever gave up. He believed in domination, total domination and when you faced him that was what you would be dealing with. He would throw resources at you continuously until he overpowered you and then dominated you. He took great pleasure in administering that last final life ending round into your head.

I turned and picked up the phone and dialed my contact at the Industrial Co-op. He came on line and we passed a couple of simple how you doing lines back and forth between one another. "Do you understand the scope of the task you have requested in regards to Mr. Stillman?"

He was listening and thinking as well. "No, I can't say I have. Why? What's the issue?"

At least he sound interested. "Well in my research I have determined this guy is one hell of a brain and he has taken the makings of that weapon with him."

I paused so my comment sunk in and then continued. "Second, when checking on Ms. Worthington, I found she is the sister of Mr. Stillman and that she was released from custody to take care of personal issues. She had left and joined her brother."

That seemed to strike a key with my contact. "She left and joined with Stillman?"

"Yeah, that's what I said. Besides Mr. Stillman has hired one Iddings Quinton as his security protection."

There was silence on the other end. "And who is this Quinton person?"

I almost laughed at his response and then continued. "Mr. Quinton, we call him Teacher, is one of the best if not the best contractor out there. I'm even having second thoughts about taking him on.

"I'm almost certain he knows about me, has done his research, and it was done in depth. He takes nothing for granted and when he moves on you, he holds nothing back. It's either all or nothing." I was getting a little irritated by this time as well.

He finally made a noise that told me he could see and understood the issue. "That means Mr. Stillman has top security, his sister has joined him and he has the potential of using that weapon system wherever and whenever he wants."

"That is right and I would suggest we take every bit of it seriously."

There was another pause. "Mr. Wicked are you telling me you want to back out of the contract with us?"

That was something I had considered, but that was not what I was calling him about. "No, I don't want to back out. In fact, I plan on going right at them and settling this thing once and for all. I don't know if this means anything to you, but when I'm challenged, I take it and go for it. No, I'm in this to the end."

I heard him breathe out. "All right Mr. Wicked, what is it you want?"

"I want absolute and total control of this issue and the go ahead to do whatever I deem necessary to end this issue in favor of our contract. I need your approval I have complete and total decision-making authority on this contract. If not then I must withdraw even though I don't want to."

"Mr. Wicked, would you stand by a moment?"

I could see him reaching over to the other phone to call his superior. He couldn't make that decision and had to go higher up. I knew by the fact he wanted to contact his higher ups told me he was taking what I had said seriously.

Finally, he came back to me. "Mr. Wicked your contract has been up graded to give you full and complete authority in all decision aspects of this issue at hand. The Co-op agrees with your assessment of the situation and they release you to carry out your contracted objective by whatever means you deem necessary with prejudice."

They were giving me everything. That was something few contractors got; it was a complete release to address the problem. They understood the issue and knew the potential for this thing to get out of control was great. "Thank you and I will keep you fully informed of what is happening and every other detail as they develop."

That ended the contact and I had received exactly what I wanted and needed. Mr. Stillman may have a strong organization and position, but it was no way near the position I was in, it was now the world against Stillman and I felt confident the world was going to win out.

It's not easy to disappear in the world. No matter how hard you try there is always something that will give you away. A single person can hide for a considerable period of time, but by shear chance alone they are usually found out. In Stillman's case he had a whole organization that needed to be hidden and that was nearly impossible.

It took me three days to locate them and then another three days to determine their level of security. It was extensive. Quinton was doing well in his job, but as with any situation such as this he could not plug all the holes. They probably knew they could not totally hide but they probably were only trying to gain time and they did just fine.

Time, yeah that's what Stillman needed. With time he could develop and build one or two weapons. He also needed a location for the project and then a facility to house and setup his weapons. That meant he had to have a fairly large area to work in, an area that was isolated and secure from ease of access.

I wasn't planning on an attack by a number of associates and me, nor a large military style attack. No, I decided on a one-man attack. That would be harder to detect and, in many respects, harder to deal with. My problem was I didn't know how well Teacher knew me. If he had concentrated on me, he would understand why I selected a single man attack. I was betting he didn't think I was that foolish.

I don't care how carefully you plan and research there is just that element of the game that is pure chance. I knew that and so did Teacher. In fact, I was depending on it this time. We would see. One thing I was sure of, this was going to be one hell of an event.

I had located Stillman and his organization in a small village in northwestern Mexico normally referred to as the Baja. The area of this small village was flat and sandy. There was little foliage or cover so when one does approach, they will be in the open almost all the way. There was only one covered approach and that was in the dark.

One man in the dark of night could and would make the assault on their stronghold. The question is. Have they prepared for it? I would find that out in time. Time, yeah, that was the key and the longer I took the closer Stillman came to completing his weapon build and the building of the facility for it. No, this was time critical and I could not waste a second.

My first job was to move south and set up a base of operations. The maps indicated the areas around the village did have mountains and they were within a reasonable distance of the village. The only problem was the direct approach to the village, but if I set up my base in the mountains, I had a direct view of the village and I could take all the time I wanted watching and learning.

But first there is one issue that needed to be handled and that was the hit team or contractor who was working me there in Detroit. Of course, there was, Teacher was not dumb and he knew I was coming so he took direct action to stop me. There had to be someone locally who had been contracted to take me out. I know if I was in Teachers place, I would do anything I could to take out any opposition before it became a problem.

There would be; no there was a contractor set up on me right now and I needed to deal with that. I didn't need someone running my back while I'm trying to deal with Stillman and his group. So, the smart thing to do is take each task as it presents itself and the contractor working that contract on me had to come first.

The next question was who and where was he or them? I went back to the contractor listing again and managed to find another missing contractor from the available listing. He was nothing big, but if I had not recognized the probability of Teacher's actions, I could have fallen victim to his hired gun.

His name was Daniel Larson, better known as 'Showboat'. He was not particularly well known but he was a stable and dependable contractor. I noted he was a loner and seldom worked with anyone else or any group. Everything I could find out about him told me he was good and planned well. This was priority one before I could go after Stillman. Showboat was now my number one issue and all else depended on my taking him down first, the sooner the better. Time, it's always time.

I was sure Teacher set this up and he would have provided everything he had on me and how I worked. That left me at a disadvantage in that I knew little about Showboat, so it's back to the computer and doing my research.

As it turned out Showboat was just what his name indicated, he was a show no matter where he went or what he was doing. He dressed the part and drove the most expensive cars. He always had an entourage with him when he moved around town, but when carrying out a contract he was almost invisible. Yet, Showboat still stood out in the way he brought about one's demise.

From that moment on I was in hunter mode and I set to work making preparations to take Showboat on. My plan was to take him out and then immediately leave this region and head for Stillman's location. In other words, I was going to drop out of sight. The plan was to sever all ties to the Detroit area at the same time going completely undercover.

I had little trouble finding Showboat when he got to town, he was at one of the best hotels in the city and he had his usual entourage with him. Clearly, he was not ready to start to work and that made him vulnerable for a direct and immediate attack. You never give the other side a break once you know they are the other side. And so, I was going to hit him before he could set up for dealing with me.

I figured I had maybe twelve hours before I needed to act or he would be into his stalking mode and I would have to deal with him on that basis. I decided on a long distance hit and set up on the roof top of a building across from the hotel where he was staying. I had his car located and set up on it. The range was perfect for the shot and I knew I would take him with a single round.

Sure, enough he and three of his associates left the hotel walking toward the car. He was easy to spot and I set in on him. Just then something told me to hold up. I zoomed in on him and recognized the man I targeted was not him. I dropped and rolled and then dropped behind a vent unit.

The first round hit just about where my head had been. Damn he had me cold. I had a good idea as to where he was, but I didn't know if he was alone or had others with him. The next round came in right behind me as I kept rolling and moving away from my original position. I knew he had me spotted and was working me.

It was then I realized he wasn't on the roof with me he was shooting from another building roof or room and it had to be across the street from my position judging by the position of the hits.

My position was untenable and I had to get the hell out of there. I moved up against the wall toward his position and worked my way around and then back to the roof entrance. That entrance would put me in direct line of fire and so far, I had a fairly good idea he was waiting for that exact shot.

I set myself up and then made the move. I had to keep moving and not give him a still target. I had but seconds and I had to make my move good. I went for it and made the door and had it open and through it. By the time the first round hit, I was in the stairwell and heading down.

Damn he had me cold and I fell right into it. I underestimated his skills and now I'm paying for it. I was sure there would be others waiting for me somewhere below and I started to work my way out of the place. I was taking the back stairways down and figured they would be somewhere on the second floor, I had two to go.

I kept moving and at the same time pulling my back pack and opening it getting ready to hit them with my fragmentation grenades. Finally, as I approached the stairs from the third floor I slowed down and eased into the stairwell. The stairs from each landing went down and turned two times to the right. I got to the first turn and then moved down to the second turn and stopped. Yeah, they were there, it sounded like two.

I pulled the pin on the first grenade and then tossed it around the corner and down the stairs. They were already scrambling when they saw my hand and the grenade coming out of it, but it was too late. It went off over their heads and that ended it.

I moved back up to the third floor and then to the back hall and out the window onto an adjoining roof and then across that roof and down to street level and into my car and headed out of town. I had a lot to think about that evening. I had misread Showboat completely. There was something really bad going on here. He knew where I was at. Damn I've been through this once before and I sure as hell didn't think I had fallen into the same trap a second time. No, there was something else here and I had better find it out.

Damn, he had me cold. He knew I was on the roof and that told me he had an inside knowledge or something on me but what the hell was it. I decided to drop my car and bring out another in the off chance the car itself was bugged. I then continued home and set up there to figure this thing out.

I had underestimated Showboat and now I knew why he was the way he was. It was a front, a means of drawing an opponent's attention away from the real threat and concentrating on his appearance, forgetting about his skills and he was skilled. Maybe he was a bad shot, but skilled none-the-less.

I still could not figure how he had spotted me. He knew I would be there and he set his team up to draw my attention away from him. Then it entered my mind maybe he was not the shooter but was the bait all along. If that was true then he had more balls than I credited him for. That was it that was the game he had set himself up as the target and I went for him. Radical as hell but it almost worked. Lesson learned.

I was ready for a second shot at him and this time it would score and I would be the aggressor. This time I planned on taking his entire entourage out at the same time. Every one of them down to the last person was marked. I couldn't let one of them walk, it was that important. I had developed the impression he was a lone worker. That his entourage was just that, a group of people he kept around him and traveled with him. My research saw them, the entourage as just that, but now I knew they were an active part of his organization, a hit team.

I changed to another car again and this time I moved out to scout my opponent in detail. I finally located them at an all-night restaurant not too far from their hotel and then set up on them. I tracked and identified each one of his people taking photos of each one and learning as much about them as I could. In checking his past contracts with the Co-op,

I learned the names and history of each of his people. He had one hell of a good crew.

I then started to prioritize each one moving from the most talented to the least. There they were. The whole team and they were a good one. I had to admit.

Now the planning, and this time it would be total and complete removal. I had my primary mission waiting for me and I needed to get on them as soon as possible.

It took me three days to set it up and finally I had them tracked and nailed to their normal activities. When on a contract they always moved together. They may split up while carrying out the plan but when moving around to a contract job or away they always stayed together.

The word came to them I had been to the Co-op and had just left and was headed east on the main drag. They thought I was going back to the Detroit Industries building to see if I could find anything on the movements of Stillman. When I got there, they were waiting and it was just as I had set it up. They knew I would come in from the back side of the building and they had set the whole street up for the showdown.

I left my car three blocks over and then moved down into the subbasement area. The city was honeycombed with tunnels running from one building to the next and I had learned well how the system worked when I was setting up the Saturn building. So, when I came in at the center of the Detroit building, they had not expected that.

The first two took it right after I came out of the stairwell from the basements. As I had suspected, they were not ready for me to come up in the middle of them. I had three to go plus Showboat and I planned on him going last. The next one tried to rush me and I put him down with a head shot.

That left two and Showboat. I moved back into the stairwell and moved up to the second floor. I heard them coming up after me and I set the door to the second floor with a fragmentation and then moved down the hall to the next stairwell. I entered the stairwell and waited. Fifteen seconds later the fragmentation at the other stairwell went off. I waited ten seconds and then moved back into the hall and back to the first stairwell. Yeah, they were there but in no mood to fight now or ever again.

That left Showboat and I headed back downstairs via the front stairwell. I waited at the door trying to determine who was in the main hall just outside the stairwell door. There was nothing at first and then I heard him. It was a quiet controlled sound of someone moving along a wall sliding with each step. He was heading right toward me.

I had figured his car was out front and he was going to try and make it there. I reached over and slowly turned the lock on the door and then settled back to let him move by. Less than ten seconds later I saw someone try the stairwell door and I put my ear against the wall and listened to him sliding on down the wall toward the main lobby area.

I charged down the stairs to the basement parking level and then sprinted toward the front of the building. I reached the pedestrian door to the parking basement and moved through that door and into the landscaping just outside the door.

There was the car sitting across the street. I could hear him running down the steps of the front entrance and when he hit the sidewalk I moved out onto the street. He was half way across the street when he saw me and that brought him to a stop. He turned toward me and stood there watching me.

I had him and he knew it. Seldom do contractors face off like this, one on one face to face. As a matter of fact, I had never faced off with anyone in this manner. It made me think of those old-time stories where gun fighters faced off against one another. So here we are facing one another down and only one would walk away.

There is a time in situations like this where you know you're going to walk away from this situation whole and I was feeling that way now. I had him and he knew it and no matter what he did I was taking him down. It was then he called out. "Do we really what to do this?"

I said nothing, just stood there watching him and waiting for him to make his move.

He was standing his ground but I could also see he didn't want to go through with this either. "Come on Denton, this is stupid. There is no need for us to continue on with this show. You took my team out and it's all over now. Just drop it and I'll be on my way."

He was giving me an out and it was one I would not be taking. This had to end with one of us not walking away and it was going

264

to be him. "Sorry Showboat but that's not possible. You're in a situation where I can't let you go. You know too much and that means I have to close this security leak, that being you."

I could see his shoulders slump with those words. I had him on the down side and he clearly doubted his abilities and that gave me the advantage. "You're not going to drop this are you?"

I shook my head no.

"I figured as much. At least I gave it a try. So, how do you want to go about this? We stand here until we're tired of one another and then draw and shoot?"

I was watching his hands and they were moving into position. "No, I'll just shoot you down."

He went for his gun but he was too late. I already had mine out and leveled on him. He froze and then realized the end was here and so he tried to finish the draw. I fired three times and two hit the mark. He went down in a heap and never moved again. I turned and headed back to my car, now it was time to deal with Stillman.

I had little time and a lot to do before I went south and took the Teacher and his crew on. I felt sure my planning was right on, a one-man attack would be the best all around. I had no doubt Teacher would set things up to deal with a team or a larger force, and that was want I wanted him to expend his time and energy on. Everything was set and it was time to go.

Two weeks later I had made it down to the Baja and moved into a cave in the mountain nearby. I was working out of a small camp to the east of the village. The mountains I had selected were the closest to the village and the elevation gave me an excellent view of the entire village and approach to it.

My approach to the area of the village had to be from a direction that would not draw their attention. Just east of the village was a bridge and the road from that bridge went right into the village proper and would have exposed my presence. So, I came in from the next bridge access further south on the east side of the mountain range. In that way I was able to work my way up to the area of the village and not be observed at any time.

I parked my rig in a small grove of trees and then packed my supplies and equipment into the area of the cave. It took me all day to make the move and once settled in I was ready to start my campaign against the Stillman group.

As I started my observations, I noted the lack of activity in the village itself. There was little going on in most of the village except for an area on the west side. There was a considerable amount of construction going on there. It didn't take long to determine the reason for the lack of activity in the village was because Stillman and his team were using the villagers as labor for this building project and I'm sure it was not voluntary labor.

After a few minutes I spotted several observation posts on the roofs of several of the village buildings. I counted four observation posts and all four were positioned to observe the south, east and north approaches to the village. From what I could tell they had men manning the observation posts but they also had automated spotting equipment at each post.

They had the main approaches to the village well covered day and night. As I watched their activity, I was able to make a determination as to how many of his people were there. It was an estimate but I counted twenty-three for sure and he may have five or six others I would classify as security. Overall, I would estimate there were at least forty people there. I was sure Teacher was in charge of the security.

I knew what Teacher and Bradley looked like, but I had no idea what Stillman looked like. I could not find any photos of him in my research. Clearly, he was photo shy and had been most of his adult life. Still, I felt it wouldn't be too difficult to separate him from everyone else when the time came.

I sat back in my position, which was actually just about perfect. I had found a cut in the ridge of a mountain that gave me cover from the sun most of the day. The back of the cut angled down into a cave and that gave me the ability to pull back and down as the sun moved directly west of me. The last thing I needed was a reflection being spotted by the observation posts.

I spent my mornings and afternoons doing observations of the village until the sun had moved to the West causing me to pull back into the cave, keeping cool and avoiding light reflections. After dark I would again move to the cut and set up and observe the village and any activity going on there.

It was in the evening when I noted that during the night time hours Teacher would send out three-man squads to walk the south, north and east regions out about a quarter mile to insure there were no intruders setting up on them.

Let's see, from my position I was at least a half mile from the village. That gave me a good comfort zone to work in. I was also a half mile from the ocean in that position which meant I could make a run around their perimeter to the ocean side and move in close for a more detailed study on what they were doing. I planned the trip the following night and set things up for a ten-hour run.

As I scanned the terrain between my position and the beach to the south, I saw I could move all the way across to the beach using a series of gullies that ran across the line of sight from the village. Once on the beach side of the village I could use the beach dunes as cover as I moved in closer. Again, I would need to be careful not to walk into a trap. Just because it looked open did not mean it was.

The following morning as I prepared for that nights scouting mission, I was looking the terrain over in the area of my first scouting mission when I spotted deep marks in the sand perpendicular to the water line. Something had been dragged out of the water and up toward the village at night. meant they were working the beach side at night as well. Hell, he had more than forty people there, he had an army.

I decided to cancel the scouting mission and concentrate on watching the water line through night vision equipment. The day passed without any significant issues being observed. As night settled in, I prepared for the observation activity.

It was just after midnight when I spotted the first activity. About a dozen men were moving out of the village and down to the water line. They stopped there and one held up what appeared to be a light and then they all waited.

Ten minutes later I spotted a wake line of something coming in toward them. Within minutes a boat came into view and started to off load a number of boxes. I could not tell what they were but they were being handled carefully. Each box was carried by two men. Half a dozen boxes were off loaded and then the boat went back out into the surf and disappeared into the darkness.

They really had this area tied down, but I have never been blocked out of any area I wanted to be in, and this was not going to be any different. I needed to get in close and find out what the hell they were up to. The scouting mission was set for the next night and I wanted to be at the beach when the boat came back, if it did.

As I sat there mulling over this new development it dawned on me this was a much bigger involvement than I had first thought. If there were boats working off shore then it meant this was probably an inter-industrial cooperation. But how could that be? Stillman was wanted everywhere, and he was thought to be a danger to the entire worldwide industrial system.

I could feel the creep running up my back. We had understated this man and under estimated what he could do or was capable of. What I was seeing here in this part of Mexico was only the beginning. If they were successful in what they were trying to setup and do, then it meant they would have support from elsewhere in the world to complete their plans.

All right, they were more than I had anticipated, so what. I still had a contract to take this man and his organization out and that's what I would be doing. I had most of what I needed and if I needed more, I could adjust my planning to take it into account.

Then it entered my mind 'overkill'. I knew when I hit them it had to be so huge and so heavy, they couldn't react or overcome the assault. It was a case of overkill. I had to hit them with so much weaponry they had no way to defend themselves. Next, and this was the most difficult, I had to include the villagers in the assault. I couldn't take their safety or survival into account.

I was faced with two choices, the world or the people of that village and the village lost. With that I set my mind to the attitude every soul I met in the village when the attack started was the enemy and everyone would die. Once I had made the determination that was it.

Actually, it wasn't a choice. It was a foregone conclusion all would have to be targeted. I would not have the time to separate one from the other. If it moved it died. If it was seen it died. If it, in anyway, made an appearance, it died. Mr. Stillman would be held accountable for that as well. I was looking forward to that moment when I could put the final round through his head.

Yeah, it sounds cold hearted, but when you're one in a fight against numbers you have to do whatever is necessary to give yourself a chance at survival. The poor people have been forced into a slave labor situation and now they would be targeted as the enemy. There was nothing I could do. If I was to overcome these people, I had to take everyone out.

Am I having second thoughts about my actions? No, I just recognize there were those present who would be paying for their innocents. That is the nature of war, the innocent always pays the higher price. In this case, they would, but I would make sure the others, those carrying out this occupation pay in spades.

Chapter Twelve

The Assault

It was one of those nights when the moon was high in the sky and everything was lit up. It was great for seeing but hell for stealth, know what I mean. I went anyway but made sure I stayed below the line of sight of the observation posts and paid close attention to any movement around where I was moving. I worked slow and easy making sure I didn't leave a trail as I moved through the gullies.

A half mile isn't bad, but when you're moving through sand and trying to keep a low profile and not leave any tracks its time consuming. I figured I could do the half mile in two hours give or take fifteen minutes. I wasn't too far off. I got there in two hours ten minutes.

I found a spot and burrowed down into it and set up my equipment. At midnight the men came out of the village and down to the beach. I turned my attention to the water and after an hour there it was, a large ship sitting about a mile off the coast. A smaller boat left the ship and moved in toward the beach as the men on the beach shinned a light for them to follow.

As the boat beached, I could hear the people in the boat talking to the on-shore people. "This is the last of it. You should have all the cases now. The Captain said we will be shipping out as soon as this load is off loaded and we get back to the ship. Do you have anything else we need to address?"

"No, did you include the booze we asked for?"

"Yeah, it's in that small case there on top. The Captain said, enjoy it."

"Thanks, I'm sure we will. You take it easy and we'll see you in three weeks."

"Right, see you then."

As they finished off loading and the boat withdrew, I watched the boat move out and beyond the breaker line and to the ship. I then moved into a parallel course with the twelve men and the boxes. As they moved into the village, I set up about one hundred fifty yards out and sat there watching.

Three weeks? That meant they had a time schedule to do whatever it was they planned on doing. I don't know how many loads they have off loaded since they have been in this location. But by the looks of the crates the items in those crates had to be high tech and probably weapons grade.

The new construction was off to my left and was made up of what appeared to be three fair sized buildings all two stories high. They were built in a triangle with windows on the three sides of the second floors facing north, east and south. What the hell were they up to? One thing I was sure of, I couldn't let them finish those buildings or the project they were working on, whatever it was.

As the moon settled down to the west I headed back for my base. It took me three hours to get back and I made it into the cave just before sun up. As I settled back, I started to think about what was going on there in the village and I knew I had to hit them soon.

If they had the weapon, I knew it could strike out and hit any point in the world from wherever it was at. This would fit in well with the capability and they were well along in the construction phase. It had to be stopped before they could activate it and make their first strike. Yeah, it had to be the weapon and all the tech equipment was for the construction of the weapon. I knew this, it wasn't completed yet.

Next, I knew I had to make a hit that would destroy everything including the village and the innocent who were living there, if you could call what they were enduring as living. I started to pull everything I had learned together and determined I had two weeks at the outside to take action.

It would take me a week to return to my primary base and collect what I needed to carry out the attack. Next, I had to decide if I wanted to do this thing as a loner or bring in additional contractors. My problem was the more contractors I brought in the greater the risk of being found out. I decided to go it alone.

That evening, I set out for my main base, prepping for the attack. There's only one way to hit a place like this and it's with everything you can muster. I figured it would take me three nights to set up my main charges in the village and then wait for the moonless night that was coming.

Back at my prime base I had all the explosives I would need. My problem was I was only one person and that meant I could only carry so much. As I stood there looking the supplies over, my eyes settled on three cases marked with red and yellow lettering. Those cases were the new explosives the Co-op had provided for me. When I took delivery, I was told when a two-pound charge of this stuff went off anything within a city block would go. Short of a nuclear device this stuff was the meanest stuff around.

I loaded those three cases first and the rest of the explosives I would need, and extra ammo. I then headed back for my base. It would take me three hours to get there and another three to move everything up to the base. That gave me six hours to think and I needed those six hours.

During this time, I determined what my target order of attack would be. It was obvious Teacher had to come first. I had to take out their top fighter and his immediate team. That would be tops and it would take the majority of my time. In addition, while dealing with the issue it would leave the window open for Stillman and Bradley to make their escape and would put me back to base one.

That brought me to the escape route and I was fairly sure it would be by sea. They seemed to have some level of ocean support going on and it would be sensible for them to use it as their primary escape route. There was nothing on land for them.

On the other hand, it would take time to coordinate a sea escape and once the attack is fully developed, any coordination with a ship off shore would be nearly impossible. Yes, I had to keep the possibility open, but the odds of a sea escape were appearing to be low on the scale of options for them, especially if I hit them hard and fast.

With that I determined I had to limit their routes of escape. If I could direct their movements then I could dictate where and when this game would end. I decided I wanted them to move south, along the beach. In order to do that I had to knock the bridge to the east out leaving them with just the one escape route.

One week before my attack I was back at my base. A quick check of the area found no one had been in or around the base. I moved my materials into the cave and commenced to put the assault hardware together. As I said before, I needed several nights to load up and go to the village and set up my devices.

I made my first trip two nights after my return. When I got to the village, I was shocked at the level of progress they had made. It appeared I was going to carry out my attack just in time, I hoped.

I started to plant my devices that night. I could carry two units at a time and it only took about five minutes to set them up and bury them. They didn't have to be on or against any particular target. All I had to do is get them within a fifty-to-seventy-five-foot range of the target.

The explosives I was using where the latest science had developed and with my working through the Industrial Co-op, I was able to get the military grade I wanted. Two pounds of this stuff could lay a city block into a crater seventy feet deep.

In three trips I got all six devices set and buried. That gave me one extra night to settle back and review my means of attack. It also gave me time to spot Teacher and hopefully determine if I could detect a pattern to his movements and activities during the night time hours. During these observations I saw no additional deliveries coming in on the beach and determined whatever they were, it had all been delivered.

How does a single man take on an army of forty or more well-armed men? Well first of all you have to be completely crazy to even try it. Second you have to use surprise actions in order to gain the upper hand. Your initial attack must take a significant number of the opposition out completely. I hoped my prior installed devices would fulfill that objective.

Next, I had to kill their communications capabilities. As long as they didn't know who was active or what their other elements were doing, the amount of confusion I could create would be to my benefit and not theirs.

My next move must target Teacher and I have to take him down or else they'll eat me alive. This cannot be an extended confrontation; I have to find him and take him out as soon as possible or I'll fail sure as hell.

It was around two that morning when I finally saw him. Yeah, that was him, no one else moves and looks like that. Just watching him move and the level of confidence he had in those moves caused me to admire this man.

He was good, but right now I had him. Once I saw him, I knew what his mode of operation was and that would give me the upper hand.

I was able to observe his movements for the better part of the night. As morning came, he moved out of the outskirts of the village and into the inner areas. By ten he was nowhere to be seen and had probably gone down for some much-needed sleep. He knew no attack would come during the day so he could relax and prepare for the eventual he felt would come.

That evening, as the sun went down, there was no moon. I waited till it was nearing eleven and then started out toward the village. As I approached the village I checked and armed each explosive and set their timers. I then withdrew and set up clear of the areas of the detonations. I had set the attack to start at two that morning, just the time I noted Teacher was making his rounds.

In situations like this, time just crawls and so it did this night. It was a case of patience and preparation. I was prepared, now I had to be patient. I was in the best possible position I could find to take on Teacher when he came by. My charges were set to go off when he reached that point of my attack. If they went off before he got there or after he got there then I would have to adjust to it.

It was two minutes to the detonation time when I first saw him. He was walking between observation posts and had stopped at the first one to talk to his men. I would say he was two thirds of the way to the next post when the first detonation took place.

It blew him clear off his feet. As a matter of fact, I was lying in a gully and when it went off, it half way buried me right where I was. That blast took out the post Teacher was approaching and ten seconds later the post he had just left went up. Ten seconds later the first of the three new buildings went off and was followed in quick succession by the other two buildings.

Teacher was up and moving when the second blast went off and I was right with him. I could tell there was something wrong as I watched him. He had a severe limp as he moved around where the first observation post had blown. I was moving almost parallel to him but at a slight angle so I could close in on him slowly. As he moved past the first detonation spot, I was within ten paces of him when he turned to face me.

My momentum took me the rest of the way to him and I hit him at full speed. He tried to swing on me but I had him head on and made the best of my approach. As we went down, I rolled over the top of him and came up behind him as he tried to get up. He knew I was there and managed to get ahold of my left arm and swung me around and down onto the ground coming down on top of me.

I rolled with his momentum causing him to continue on over me and on to the ground face first and with his back arched. I threw a punch and hit him in the kidney and liver area. He crumpled under the punch but still tried to come up and around on me.

With my knife in my right hand, I came on over him and trust my knife up and into his arm pit. He tried to clamp down but I penetrated about half the blades length into his body and then twisted and rocked the knife back and forth each time driving it deeper into his body.

I jerked the knife out and drove it into his side and up toward his heart. I had him now and he knew it. I was ripping his insides apart but he was not giving up. The damn fool just kept on fighting. I had to finish this now or I was going to be up to my neck in fighters shortly.

I grabbed for his head and got my hand under his chin and then drove the knife into his neck and again rocking it back and forth. I felt the blood washing over my hand and knew I had made the fatal move. I let him go and pulled the knife and rolled away from him and down into the gully. When I looked up toward the top of the gully there, he was standing there holding his throat. It was then I opened up on him with my .40 and finished the job.

By this time the other charges were going off and tearing the village apart. I moved toward the beach and then up and out of the gully and headed for the central part of town. From this point on I was shooting anything moving, whether fighter or villager.

All in all, I figured the charges had taken care of better than seventy percent of the armed fighters in the village. As the battle continued, I don't know how many of the villagers fell victim to the fighting. The further I moved into the village the less the gun fire I encountered. As I reached the center of the village I moved on through and toward the north side and the observation post there.

As I closed in, I observed the post had been effectively destroyed and I then shifted back toward the three new buildings, they were gone as well.

Call it good planning or simple dumb luck everything had worked out perfectly. Now I needed to shift my attention to Stillman and Bradley. If they survived the blast at the three buildings then they would be trying to leave the area. It was safer for them to move away from the village toward the water and then either take a boat or move north or south along the shore line.

I swung around the north side of the new buildings and headed south checking the sand for any new tracks that would tell me which direction they and gone. There were none. I then swung around the south side and prepared to turn north. So far, I had found nothing. As I moved north, I finally came to a set of tracks. There were actually five of them, four men and one woman. They were headed east and that could only mean there was a vehicle out there some place.

I stopped and listened and then got down and took a close look at the tracks. Sure, enough the sand was still settling back into them and I knew they were within a stone's throw. I dove to the left hit the ground and rolled as several rounds came in on me. I came around and sent a dozen rounds back in the direction theirs came from.

I could hear them scrabbling but there were only three sets of feet moving. That meant two were staying behind to try and take me out or delay me. If they could slow me down the others had a good chance of getting away.

It was time and I reached into my pocket and pulled out my cell phone. I hit the code and three miles away the bridge, the only bridge out of this region went up. That put them between me and the river. They had only the three ways to go, toward the river, which they would now abandon, north toward the border, or south, deeper into the Baja.

The border was on high alert by now so they really only had one way to go and that was south. I heard the engine start and the vehicle pull away and then turn south. I still had two more here to deal with and then I would be after them.

I figured the other two would split up and try to get me between them. That was alright with me I only needed to deal with one at a time and when they split that helped. I rolled on over half a dozen more times and then got up and sprinted north to the first dune and stopped. I heard his steps as he moved along parallel to me and when I stopped, he did the same.

I lay back against the dune and then pushed myself backward up the dune staying flat on my back. Halfway up I stopped and half buried myself in the sand and stayed put. I could hear him moving along the bottom of the dune and when he was right below me, I sat up and ran a line of shots down the dune right on top of him. He grunted and I heard him hit the ground. At the same time, I was rolling across the face of the dune and down toward the bottom as the rounds came in from the other side of the road.

I moved away from the dune and crossed the road and set up for the last man. He had been running hard and had circled back and was coming almost directly at me. I could hear his heavy breathing. He was getting fatigued now and that made him careless. He almost ran right into me. By the time he saw me it was too late and I put him down.

It was three quarters of a mile from my position to my base and I knew Stillman would be way ahead of me, heading down the Baja. It was over a hundred miles to the next bridge heading east and I knew he was trying to make it there. I started to run and set everything else out of my mine. I need to get to my rig and move out now.

As I climbed up to my base, I looked south and there he was. I could see their head lights moving south along the base of the mountain range. I had it pegged right. They were heading for the next bridge.

I figured there were three of them in the car Stillman, Worthington and their bodyguard. Bradley was probably not a physical hazard to me, so that left Stillman and the bodyguard. I knew the bodyguard would be trained and probably the most lethal. Stillman was an unknown and so I had to consider him as dangerous.

I got to the cave, got the rest of my gear and ran to my rig and headed south on the east side of the range. They had a hundred miles to run and I had only eighty-two and it meant I could be there waiting for them. It was going to be close, but I knew I had them. It was just a matter of time.

By sun up I was sitting at the east to west road about five miles from the bridge waiting for them to come. If everything went right, they would have to come past me right here. I could hear the car before I saw it. As it rounded the bend I stepped onto the road and readied myself. He was near full throttle when he came around the curve and saw me. He never slowed for a second and I opened up on him when he was about fifty yards from me.

The last twenty-five yards the car was being driven by a dead man. It slipped by me at about forty miles an hour when it ran off the road and into the ditch. I ran to the car and when I got there and looked inside there was only one occupant and he wasn't Stillman. They had taken two cars and one followed with its lights out. I saw the one set of lights and determined they were all in one car. That mistake was mine.

I stood there looking back up the road when I caught a small flash of light. It was up at the top of the pass right in the road cut. Someone was watching me and they were waiting to see what I would do once I found just the one person in the car. I immediately ran across to my rig and jumped in and drove across the road and headed south on the eastern road toward the next bridge.

Once out of view of the vehicle at the pass, I stopped and ran back to the road and took a position in the rock along the side of the road. Sure, enough here they came. As they came up alongside me, I stood up and opened up on the front and rear tires. The first rounds hit the engine and then tore into the tires both front and rear.

It had gone completely quiet not a sound was heard not even the wind. I waited and watch the car to see if there was any action inside. With what I knew about Bradley, I could see her sitting there with a booby-trap waiting for me to come up to the car and look in. They were dead in the water and just sat there. I stayed put and waited for them to exit the car. Finally, they came out and stood there looking back toward where I had been. "I'm not there you two."

They both started to swing around. "Hey don't you move another inch. Stay just as you are and I'll tell you when to move."

They slowly raised their hands and then Ms. Worthington started to turn around. I let her. "Mr. Wicked you never give up do you?"

I smiled at the fact she had the guts to make the turn back toward me. "No Bradley I never do."

She lowered her hands. "Where do we go from here?"

"That, young lady, should be obvious. You both die here and now. That's what the contract calls for and what I'll deliver."

Her expression didn't change one iota. "What would it take to pay you for our lives?"

Man did she have the balls. "Sorry Bradley I can't do that. I have a reputation to maintain and beside you've been one hell of a pain in the neck for me these past few months."

During this exchange Stillman had not moved an inch. He just stood there looking down the road. I called out. "Mr. Stillman you can turn around now."

He didn't move for several seconds and then slowly he started his turn. As he came around, I saw something I had never anticipated. He had no face. There was a hole where the nose should have been. No eyes and just a small part of a mouth, as best as I could see he did not have any teeth. His ears were just buttons on the side of his head. This was the man who had brought all this mayhem and death upon this region over this past year. There was something really wrong here.

I looked at Bradley. "All right Bradley what the hell is going on here?"

"Mr. Wicked, he's a genius but he can't communicate as other do. I have been his mouth for years and I am also his brain trust. We have been keeping this secret for years. He stayed home and I worked in his place. I became aware of his skills and started to take advantage of them and then I saw the opportunity of a lifetime to really make his life pay off for him."

I was looking at this young woman who had become her brother's keeper and she had gone too far. She was insane and had caused the death of all those people because of a missed sense of honor for her brother. "No Bradley, none of this was for him, it was all for you. You have spent your life caring for him and once you discovered his real abilities you took advantage of him. You're evil beyond comprehension and I should have killed you in Dearborn. I'll live the rest of my life regretting that."

With that she clinched her fist and start screaming at me. "You fool, can't you see what I have here. I hold the world in my hands and its people like you who continually try to take it away from me. Well not any more. My brother is mine and no one else will profit from him. I am going to rule the better part of this world and there's nothing you or anyone else can do about it."

Well, she knew what she wanted but she had forgotten one small detail, I was going to kill her. "Bradley, listen to me, this is going to end right here and now. You're not going to go anywhere from here, it's time to die."

She was still standing there looking at me and turning her head side to side as if she was trying to get a better look at me. By this time, I was walking up to her and just ten steps away when she came at me. I grabbed her and spun her around and placed my arm around her neck. "Sorry Bradley but this is the way it has to be. I wish it could have been some other way."

With that I snapped her neck and let her settle down at my feet. I looked over at Stillman and pulled my .40 and shot him in the chest dead center. It was all over. I had completed my contract and the system would return back on track to normalcy.

I stood there looking down at Bradley. Now she looked like a small innocent child laying there in the dirt of the road. There was a small smudge of dirt on her cheek. I bent over and wiped the dirt off of her face and then arranged her clothes so she looked more presentable.

Somehow, she had become her brother's keeper. I don't know if it was by choice or because of a sense of loyalty and love. What I did know was it had been too much for her and her mind failed her and she almost took the world with her.

I returned to my rig and made the call, turned around and pulled back on to the road. I turned right and drove around Bradley's body and headed back home. I left the two of them there in the middle of the road for the satellites to scan and confirm the job had been done. I was never informed as to what had happened to their bodies.

Four days later I was walking into the head office of the Industrial Co-op. The Chairman of the Co-op met me at the reception desk and we went to his office. It had been a long six months working this contract and I needed some time off. He sat back in his seat and reached out and slid a check across the desk to me. As I picked it up, I read the amount. I looked at him and he nodded. "It's just a little bonus for a job well done."

I nodded and stood up as he reached out to shake my hand. He reached down and picked up an envelope and handed it to me. "Open this when you get home. I think you'll find this good reading."

We shook hands again and I then left the office returning to my car and heading out of town to my man cave. I was more than a little wealthy at this time and I decided I needed to take a break. I set my message system up with an alert I was out of the office for a couple of months and would not be available for any contracts.

This contract had taken a lot out of me. Unlike most contracts, this one was prolonged and extremely violent. A lot of people and contractors had died during the implementation of the contract from Detroit Industries and my contract with the Industrial Co-op. For the first time I felt tired and a little more worn than I normally felt after completing a contract.

I made a cup of coffee and found a package of cookies and sat down at the table. My whole body seemed to wilt at that point. The thought crossed my mind I may not want to work another contract the rest of my life. I knew it was just fatigue and maybe it wasn't. Just maybe I was feeling my mind and soul telling me it was time to stop and do something else. I don't know. I'll just leave that decision for later on, after I'm more myself and not some punched out being.

I picked up the envelope and opened it and pulled out a stack of pages. The first page was titled Jacobi and Bradley. I started to read. "Mr. Wicked this is a report on the back ground of Jacobi and Bradley. It is meant to give you the information you need in order for you to understand what took place and to help you set it aside and behind you.

"As you know, the two were brother and sister with Bradley being the youngest. At birth Jacobi was born without a face. He had no eyes at all, just a hole where his nose should have been, a small opening for a mouth with no teeth and both ears were just buttons.

"It had been recommended the parents euthanize Jacobi at the time but both parents refused and they took their child home. From that point on Jacobi was kept in isolation by his parents as a means of protecting him from the difficulties of life.

"Two years later Bradley was born and in time she became connected with Jacobi and spent the rest of her life living for him. What the parents did not know was Bradley had developed an understanding of just how intelligent Jacobi really was.

"With his brain locked inside that head and with no way to communicate, no one knew how far advanced his mind was. That is until Bradley came along. There was some inherent connection between the two that gave Jacobi the ability to communicate with Bradley, and that communication could take place whether they were side by side or miles apart.

"As they grew up, the connection increased to the point their two minds were almost in a state of melding together. That is when Bradley entered Jacobi in school and started his education. She had to prove to the school administration she actually could communicate with Jacobi and she was successful in the process.

Over the next fifteen years she would take him through three PhD degrees. During the final years, as he was completing the third degree, she went on a recruitment mission to get Jacobi, the two of them, a job in development and design. That's when she met Mr. Worthington of PowerHouse Industries. They were hired and Jacobi started to produce.

"It was during the development of the new power generator Bradley made the move on PowerHouse Industries, and the board of directors of the company were eliminated one at a time in manners that appeared to be natural or accidental, including the owner Mr. Worthington.

"Bradley took over and infused her first name into the Worthington name and became the Chairman of the Board with a new handpicked board she had set up. At the time the name PowerHouse was changed to Saturn Futures.

"At the same time, Jacobi had developed the weapons system and Bradley knew she had to have a larger company backing the development, so she went to Detroit Industries. She hit total success when demonstrating the power unit to their board and they agreed to a partnership.

"That was when the board of directors of the Detroit Industries started to die out, as did their Chairman. Bradley moved Mr. Costello in as the new Chairman and brought the Saturn Futures Board over to Detroit Industries and the takeover was complete.

"Mr. Wicked, the manner in which Bradley carried out these take overs were nothing but mind boggling. We eventually learned with her mind and Jacobi's working together they made up a super brain and it gave them the ability to carry out their actions.

"The Co-op knew there was a serious problem and risk of total worldwide domination by Bradley and Jacobi if something was not done and done soon. We either stopped them or there was going to be a war unlike any war in the history of mankind. That is when you were brought into this issue. You know the story from then on except for one thing.

"The village was their next step to gain world domination. It was a last chance action, if successful, would have brought the rest of the world under their domination. That location gave them the ability to set up the super weapon and then take the rest of the industrial world out.

"If that weapon had gone on line, we would have never been able to stop them. Once activated it would generate its own power shield. Nothing the rest of the world had could have penetrated it. Bradley could have then picked us off one at a time and eventually taken us all.

"It was that close. You successfully carried out your contract and that is why you found the bonus attached. We fully understand the difficulty of this contract. Again, thank you."

I set the letter down and then leaned back in my chair. She had been one hell of an evil little thing hiding behind her youth and beauty, and I fell for it. Well, it's over now and I can take some time off. I would imagine the rest of the world will breathe a sigh of relief knowing for the time being Wicked wouldn't be wicked any more.

As I sat there, a thought came to my mind. Was Bradley bad or was she controlled by Jacobi. He needed eyes and ears and a mouth to speak through. His mind was beyond anything this world had ever experienced and through that and his relationship with Bradley he could control everything.

Yes, Bradley was crazy, but she had been driven there by the domination of Jacobi's mind over hers. The evil was not

Bradley it was Jacobi all the time. With her he had complete and total access to the world outside his own physical ability to function. Once he had made the connection with Bradley, he then controlled and directed her to carry out his bidding. No Bradley was crazy, but she was driven there by her brother and that was the foundation of her destruction.

This started out as a mutually beneficial system between them and had turned in to a situation of domination and destruction for both of them. Jacobi deserved to die. With Bradley it had become a necessity. She could never have lived without Jacobi.

I couldn't help but think of the friends I had lost during this contract. What was even more difficult was the fact I had been the tool used to eliminate them. I guess that's part of the game. You work in this field and you die there as well. Each had a choice and each took their respective choice they were willing to live by. In actuality they died by it. As a result, the world lost half a dozen good contractors all for the sake of power. Now that's just wicked.

www.ingramcontent.com/pod-product-compliance
Lightning Source LLC
Chambersburg PA
CBHW070831250626
47159CB00003B/727